# Goes On, Without the World's Understanding

**THOMAS WESTERFIELD**

Rattling Good Yarns Press
33490 Date Palm Drive 3065
Cathedral City CA 92235
USA
www.rattlinggoodyarns.com


Library of Congress Control Number: 2023934522
ISBN: 978-1-955826-36-5


First Edition

*To Stewart and Peaches, with a beatific smile*

# Contents


Thoughts _______________________________________________ 1

Surviving ______________________________________________ 4

Mr. Sissy in Sin City____________________________________ 20

The Barbies in the Closet _______________________________ 32

Today's Agenda ________________________________________ 42

American Horror Story __________________________________ 60

This is Enough _________________________________________ 62

Obituaries ____________________________________________ 70

Andrew _______________________________________________ 81

The Boy in the Audience_________________________________ 92

Ideal Lover Wanted ____________________________________ 103

The Last Great Aria of a Magnificent Faggot _____________ 105

His Father _____________________________________________ 121

Acknowledgments ______________________________________ 134

About the Author ______________________________________ 137

Boom. Goes on without the world's understanding. The heart can't wait. Revolts without understanding. Boom. Goes on. Without the world's understanding...

~"Oriflamme," short story by Tennessee Williams, written in January 1944 and first published in *Vogue,* 1974

# Thoughts



*Stop thinking these thoughts!*

You are here. You are there. You are running. Everything is happening so fast.

Yet everything feels slow and heavy. It is as if you are moving through something thick. Something below the surface of things. At the same time, you are watching all that is happening from far above. You are an audience worried about the scene you see yet weirdly calm at the same time.

*I am all over the place. Neither here nor there but everywhere.*

*Such a stupid thing to think right now.*

You race to the door, then help push old, faded furniture out of the way so the ambulance people can get a stretcher inside the small living room that announces your family's poverty. A slender, dainty glass flower holder with three snow-white daisies—your mother's attempt towards beauty, a touch of pride—is knocked over on the cheap forest-green carpet, always rough and wiry under your bare feet.

*Blood leaping. Jetting! Kind of like come when you jerk off.*

*Why am I thinking that?*

You are shouting, directing them down a thin, tight hallway wallpapered with something that may have once been pretty, even delicate, if one took time to really look.

Your little brother is crying, hysterical, clinging tightly to you even as you go so fast. You try to comfort him, keep him close, but also try to push him behind you, so he does not see.

*Do not let him see the blood.*

Though you slide and fall in it. Are smeared with it.

*Do not look at the blood.*

You hold back the vomit slowly climbing its way up your throat.

Blood and shouting and the ambulance people and the police and the wreckage through the house and your brother wailing. So much burning panic. You wish you could leave your skin.

*So much of the body is liquid. Blood, tears, piss, come.*

*Crazy. I must be crazy.*

Your parents' bedroom is dingy and tiny. Made tinier now because it is so crowded with all the people, the stretcher, their lifeless bloody bodies—his on the floor, hers on the bed.

Everyone knows there is nothing that can be done. Your father can't be saved. Your mother can't be saved. But the ambulance people, for some reason, are trying. Questions are being asked by the police as you are the oldest, the one in charge now, even though you are only sixteen.

*Liquids of the body are unstoppable once they're let loose.*

*No use crying over spilt milk.*

*Don't laugh! Not now.*

*What is wrong with me?*

You can't look at the bloody bodies. You know you will throw up if you do. You might even become as hysterical as your little brother.

You talk to the police, enunciating your words with great care. Telling them of the escalating, spilling hate between your parents this morning. Of every morning.

*Body liquids can't be returned, can't flow in reverse.*

You tell the police what you witnessed. His murder.

*Deserved it.*

Your mother was swift. Plunged the knife right into his heart with a force and a fury you never ever guessed was there.

Then, just as swiftly, she turned the knife inward and shoved it into her belly, falling back onto the bed.

*Couldn't stop her. Honest.*

The police want to know who should be called. They ask if any grandparents are still alive. What about uncles?

You are scared. You know there is no money, no possible way to pay for caskets and graves and headstones. None of it can be paid for.

*Thoughts can't be stopped any more than all this wetness of the body.*

*White trash faggot.*

*Not worth shit.*

*Here's the inheritance.*

# Surviving

Dr. Miriam Birnbaum's Tuesday Evening Therapy Group for Adult Male Survivors of Childhood and Adolescent Incest and Sexual Abuse is deteriorating into chaos. And though Jonathan Lake knew that, in an essential way, Dr. Miriam Birnbaum had saved his life, he could not help but feel lightheaded, almost champagne giddy, as things spun more and more out of control. A long-corked bottle of suppressed resentments and angers was in the process of being popped, and its potential spewing out delighted him.

"It was a Southern thing," Matt Oberst, the newest and, at twenty-four, the youngest member of the group, was repeating with increased impatience.

"Just because it is a cultural norm does not make it any less abuse," Dr. M, as she prefers to be called by her clients, repeats herself in a slightly wet lisp. But Jonathan is alert to the pronounced tension beneath her usual preternatural calm.

"You can't accept that you are a victim," Martin Wagner now intruded, feigning sympathy but unable to hide his mild sneer of condescension. Martin was the longest attending member, having recently celebrated his sixth year. He was tall and skinny with frizzy gray hair that grew out in all directions despite obvious thinning patches. Indeed, the angry electricity of his hair was the most alive element of the pockmarked, sallow-skinned fifty-three-year-old man. His face, all pinched and tight angles, had the tiny scar of a prim, unhappy mouth from which low fey whines emitted whenever he spoke. Which was far too often as far as Jonathan was concerned.

"I wasn't a 'victim' of anything," Matt responds. "It only happened twice, and one of those times was because I snuck out of the house at midnight to drive around getting drunk with my friends."

"You sound like you're justifying your father's abuse," Dr. M, ever persistent, notes.

"But it wasn't abuse. That's my point. There was a reason for it. A junior in high school driving around drunk at midnight is a pretty valid reason for a spanking."

"Spankings *with a belt*," Martin maliciously underlines the detail, his whine becoming higher pitched. "And it doesn't matter if it even happened once. Abuse is abuse. You are a *victim* of abuse." He seemed almost to relish his stressing of the word "victim."

Martin had been emotionally manipulated and sexually misused by a Catholic priest as a barely pubescent child. Each year he insisted that the group lengthen its name to include "Victims" within their title: The Tuesday Evening Therapy Group for Adult Male Victims and Survivors of Childhood and Adolescent Incest and Sexual Abuse. With more passion than he ever displayed about anything else in his life, Martin doggedly advocated that embracing "victims" was a necessity for any honest acceptance of their experience. How could any of them claim the mantle of "survivor" unless they were willing to brand themselves with the prerequisite word that gave "survivors" its valid meaning?

When honest with himself, Jonathan was in general agreement with this fairly sensible point. But he refused to support Martin in his annual crusade. In part because he was indifferent to what was, for him, a pointless exercise of categorization. Nothing of his history, nothing of any of their histories, could ever be so easily reduced and encased by such bland, broad labels as "victim" and/or "survivor." But it was also a matter of principle for him to never agree with anything of the obnoxious, high-strung Martin's point of view.

Since everyone else was vehement in their refusal to accept the sticker of "victim" despite Martin's finely delineated argument, the group remained titled as it always had been. Jonathan thought Dr. M, who strictly maintained her professional detachment in not taking sides during these times of debate, was always secretly pleased with the result. Martin would concede his loss with a six-paragraph email to the group expressing his profound disappointment with them all, vociferously making his case one last time. This was followed by a wounded, sulky silence that lasted for several weeks, which frankly was a relief to all the rest of them. The issue would then lie dormant for many months, to bloom once again the following year—a sign of spring's return.

"A couple of spankings are not abuse," exasperated Matt says once more.

"Bu-but...he di-did...make you ta-take...your clothes...off." The soft-spoken, tentative Paul Keats is making a valorous effort to speak, to be a contributing member to the group, to help others. Paul, a handsome, athletic man with a sweet, winning smile in his early thirties (though he looks much younger), speaks almost less in the group than Jonathan. He is so stuttering and stammering, shy and shaky, when he talks, the anxiety he exudes is unbearably embarrassing for all of them. Everyone in the group is overwhelmed with a need to reassure and protect him.

"Which is the way boys, even teenage boys, in the South got punished," Matt sighs, once again explaining a distinction Dr. M especially seems unable to grasp. "In some places, they still do. Knowing my granddad, I'm sure my dad got it a lot worse and a lot more often than I ever did."

"Still, I...I'm sorry that it...it hap-happened to...you," Paul almost whispers, barely raising his big, childlike brown eyes to look directly at Matt. It is so easy for Jonathan to see the confused and guilt-ridden eleven-year-old boy Paul once was. A boy so self-blaming for his parents' divorce, and so determined for his mother not to ever feel such great pain again, that he never told her about the late-night rapes he endured by her second husband—the stepfather who only married her to have unfettered access to him.

Paul's genuine caring momentarily soothes Matt's mounting frustrations. He now speaks only to Paul, turning in his chair as far as is possible in the circle so that his back is to Martin, who sits to Dr. M's left. *Her ever-faithful flying monkey*, Jonathan cruelly thinks.

"Thanks, Paul. I appreciate you saying that. But those spankings weren't a big deal. They were over and done within a matter of minutes. And my dad never touched me anywhere else on my body. He didn't even touch me on the butt because he used the belt. Yeah, I was naked and yeah, I was mortified, and it hurt. But I'm not going to hate my dad. I'm not going to say he abused me, and I sure as hell am never going to say he *sexually* abused me. That's just sick."

But Martin Wagner is not about to let Matt Oberst dare define his own experience and what its meaning is for himself. "You are in total denial about what happened to you. Naked whippings by your father *is* sexual abuse," he enunciates with clipped nasally diction.

"Oh, fuck you, Martin," Matt flares.

"This is becoming difficult for you, I can see," Dr. M lightly lisps, empathetic and motherly.

"Apologize to me now!" Martin commands, inflamed with insult. Jonathan suspects an eight-paragraph email full of outraged hurt feelings is already being composed for distribution to the entire group the very first thing tomorrow morning.

"Fuck you, Martin," reiterates Matt in response. But he now says it with utter calm and cool.

"Boys! Boys!" Dr. M admonishes, alarmed at the rampant disregard for her protocols of proper group therapy behavior. "Please. You must speak to one another with respect. You cannot allow yourselves to be overrun with rancor to the point where you attack rather than support each other. Let's everyone stop for a moment. Everyone. Now. Sit up. Straight. Close your eyes."

Surprisingly, everyone immediately and obediently does as instructed. Dr. Miriam Birnbaum's seven clients in the Tuesday Evening Therapy Group for Adult Male Survivors of Childhood and Adolescent Incest and Sexual Abuse align themselves in perfect ramrod straight-back posture. *Flying monkeys, all of us*, Jonathan muses to himself. *So well trained.*

"And slowly...slowly...take a deep breath in," she firmly directs in an annoying sing-song cadence. "And slowly...slowly...let the breath out. Again. Slow. Deep. Breath. In. And, then...slow. Deep. Breath. Out."

She continues repeating this cycle of inhalation and exhalation a dozen times over. The room becomes less charged. Something that had been jarring, even panicked, is stilled. Dr. M has heroically reined them in from their own worst impulses and behaviors yet one more time.

But after everyone has opened their eyes and everything seems to be restored to equitable balance, it instantly becomes apparent that neither Martin nor Matt has been placated by breathing.

"You must apologize to me," Martin solemnly and prissily dictates.

But Matt's recalcitrance has only rooted deeper. He does not acknowledge Martin in the least. Instead, he holds his pale blue eyes directly on Dr. M's watery, slate-gray ones. "We are not boys. We are men. Stop infantilizing us."

Something implacable has overtaken him, and Jonathan is thrilled but also vaguely fearful. He is hyperaware that everyone is shifting in their seats, fully attentive—this is the first time someone in the group has challenged her calling them "boys" or made a demand upon her to change some aspect of herself for their benefit.

Dr. M absently primps her ringlets of mousey brown hair and rearranges the multicolored shawl enfolding her shoulders and wrapping across her ample bosom. "That is not my intention at all," she declares with steeled conviction.

"I came to see you because I was depressed over the breakup. That's why I came. But we never talk about Amy anymore. I never get to talk about losing her. I never get help with that at all. Instead, ever since you heard about it, you've constantly focused on the two times I ever got spankings from my dad and kept pushing me and pushing me until I finally joined this group. And so far in these two weeks that's all you'll let me talk about. Never about Amy." Matt pauses for a second, suddenly hesitant. But he plunges ahead as soon as he sees Dr. M is about to speak. "You keep wanting me to tell you the details of the spankings. Repeat them over and over again."

Dr. M is unable to prevent a startled, offended expression from crossing her face. There is another tense shifting of bodies in seats. Jonathan waits expectantly, wondering what her response will be to this treasonous observation. One he himself has made but never dared express aloud. While he knows the excruciating, horrible details must always, eventually, be spoken aloud—and yes, sometimes repeated—he has been struck, and even become suspicious, of how microscopic Dr. M's probing is on the minute particulars of each of their abuse. He has noticed how much further she leans forward in her chair, eyes alight, fascinated, even spellbound, as she avidly requests more description of the settings, the perpetrators, the acts, the sounds, the smells. Every vivid slice of it that was recorded in their mind's eyes as it happened.

But Dr. M gives the disturbing implications of Matt's indictment no acknowledgment, much less validation. Precisely matching his implacable tone, she only says, "As I have explained before, I believe your father's abuse is the true source of a depression that existed long before you ever met Amy, much less after you ended your relationship with her."

"I didn't break up with Amy. She broke up with me. You don't listen."

"I am so sorry you feel that way," Dr. M responds, ever solicitous.

"She left me. I didn't leave her. You latch on to every little detail about spankings I got nearly ten years ago, but you don't bother to remember a fact as important as that the first woman I ever loved left me. I didn't leave her. That's why I'm depressed. It has nothing to do with my dad at all."

"I know this all must feel so difficult and painful for you," Dr. M almost purrs, soft and soothing. "But your struggles of resistance are a very natural part of the therapy process."

"Anytime I point out how you're wrong, you say I'm being 'resistant,'" Matt roars. "That's just some get-out-of-jail-free card you flash to justify your own fucking incompetence."

Dr. M's eyes enlarge, pierced with shock. Her jowly dumpling face shakes, and the normally big-toothed smile collapses as both her thick upper and lower lips begin to quiver. For the first time that Jonathan can remember, her short, plump body, always held erect with poise, slumps. He is thrown by her dejection and distress and momentarily regrets his silent cheering on of all this raging discord.

"You owe Dr. M an apology. You owe me an apology. You owe all of us an apology." Martin, his hideous whine grating upon Jonathan's ears, is in high dudgeon. The eight-paragraph email must now have grown to at least eleven or twelve, Jonathan surmises, enumerating all the reasons why Matt Oberst must be expelled from Dr. Miriam Birnbaum's Tuesday Evening Therapy Group for Adult Male Survivors of Incest and Sexual Abuse.

Multiple voices come from all over the circle, nearly everyone keyed up and wanting to speak at once, most in defense of Dr. M. However, a couple of them are emboldened by Matt's confrontation to finally vocalize some of their own long-held criticisms and objections.

Jonathan, as is his wont, stays silent, surveying the room. It is his default whenever there is too much roiling temper in his surroundings. Keep quiet and observe. Stay alert to each and every individual's tone of voice, key into the slightest changes of facial expression. Carefully track all gestures and movements. These are his surveillance methods to stay out of the way of anyone's—everyone's—potential explosion into verbal and/or physical violence. Make no sound, say no word, do nothing that will bring attention. Indeed, beyond the required brief "check-in" at the top of each session where he mumbles vaguely about "how he is doing" in two minutes or less, he has said nothing during the group session for the past five weeks. Dr. M has serenely made no effort to coax him into speaking more and has mercifully left him alone.

He suddenly exchanges glances with Gary Leavitt, an extremely intelligent and successful software engineer, as well as the one person in the group that he likes and with whom he is truly comfortable. Gary widens his green eyes, then rolls them wildly, ending in a comic cross-eyed expression that drives Jonathan dangerously close to laughing out loud. Gary discreetly shakes his head and rolls his eyes again, this time frowning, and Jonathan knows the meaning of his expression: *Can you believe this shit?*

In Jonathan's estimation, Gary Leavitt is the real winner of Martin Wagner's long-running, never-ending pageant competition for the title of He Among Us Who Has Suffered the Most. Gary is the one who has gone through the worst hell out of all of them. For Gary had not received spankings but whippings, and not only on his buttocks but all over his body, and not in a matter of minutes but sometimes for an hour, and not on two occasions but so many times they could not be counted. There most certainly was touching all over his body before, during, and after, and eventually, oral and penetrative sex. That it lasted for close to seven years and until he was a sophomore in college is the source of Gary's rage and shame from which he has barely disentangled himself. That it had all been perpetrated by his mother is Gary's even greater rage and shame.

"Women get by with murder," he had bitterly spat out to Theresa, his wife, two months before they married. "They uphold this golden icon of themselves as overworked, stressed-out, abandoned wife and self-sacrificing martyred mother so that no one holds them responsible or accountable for anything."

A Chinese American woman of great good common sense and an innate ability for unassailable acceptance of life's vicissitudes, Theresa understood why her husband would think this way. Still, the toxic levels of disgust and impotent fury underlying it was not something she would have any future daughter or son be exposed to, nor would she allow any seepage of it into her marriage.

Theresa told Gary she wanted him to begin therapy immediately despite how brilliantly he was progressing in his career and how over-the-moon joyous he was about their upcoming wedding. He needed to have an outlet for his volcanic and dangerous emotions and, hopefully, find a measure of resolution about what had happened to him. He could not project his feelings about his horrific past—despite how justified those feelings were—onto her or any potential offspring they would someday create. Gary needed to find a proportion that would be no more damaging than that of any other functioning adult parent upon a child. That much, at least, she thought was reasonable.

She did not have to couch her request in terms of an ultimatum. Gary knew that Theresa's great good common sense would lead her, with regret but without hesitancy, to leave his sorry ass if he did not go into therapy. She was too much of a miracle in his life to ever risk losing.

Gary is the only one Jonathan speaks to or spends time with outside of the group. They started individual therapy with Dr. M at the same time two years ago. Scheduled back-to-back, they developed a nodding waiting room acquaintance as well as an intuitive reading of each other's weekly emotional temperature through facial expressions and body language as Gary left his appointment and Jonathan was about to enter his. Joining the Tuesday group eight months later, they became fast friends.

Theresa adores Jonathan. It's also part of her great good common sense that she knows, along with a skilled female therapist, Gary is in need of at least one close male friend. She is grateful for their bond. Besides the Tuesday evening therapy group, Gary and Jonathan spend most Thursday nights together, giving her a few hours off from being a full-time wife with a full-time career as a dentist. Their hanging out allows her to get cozy on the sofa and watch the TGIT line-up of television shows that begins with her all-time favorite, *Grey's Anatomy*, and, until her recent pregnancy, having a couple of glasses of wine while doing so. She knows Gary is in good, safe hands with Jonathan.

At the same age of thirty-four, Jonathan and Gary are more honest with each other than anyone else in their lives, especially about the consequences of their respective encounters with incest, what it wrecked and wrought upon their psyches and souls. Despite their differing sexualities, relationship status, and gender of incestuous parent—Jonathan being gay, single, and sexually abused by his father—they have revealed all the details of what occurred. They know the self-destructive lives they created in the aftermath as well, trying to cope with it all.

They have listened to each other with a sacred patience and compassion, never judging the other's experiences and, more so for Jonathan than Gary, of the degradations, struggles, and failures before admitting that help was required. Tears have been shared and much simple fraternal support has been offered and received. Though they would never dare speak about it for fear of its loss, they know they are the only people in their lives with whom they feel entirely safe.

So safe, in fact, that they are free to make a morbid dark-humored play at times. Leaving a voicemail to Jonathan, Gary will call out in a scared childlike voice in the dark, "Daddy? Daddy? Are you there, Daddy? I'm scared, Daddy. Where are you, Daddy?" And Jonathan will return the call with a message in the thickly caricatured Southern accent of a gruff old man ruling his patch of Tobacco Road dirt farm. "This is Big Daddy, boy. Git your nekkid ass into bed now causa Big Daddy is on his way home and wants his boy's hole all cleaned out, lubed up, and wide open, ass ready. Big Daddy's got himself a big cock for a-poundin' his little boy!"

It is the brutal, private humor of men who have been in war and seen things and done things no one, especially ones who started out so young and innocent, should ever have to see and do. Being able to trade such knowing outrageousness makes them both laugh uproariously. Despite some shame and embarrassment, it creates an exorcising spirit releasing horrors only they would ever know, bonding them even further into friendship.

Both know Dr. M would find such humor "problematic," her code word translating into, "This is wrong. I disapprove. Stop it." Or they would be given a lengthy, gently spoken, patronizing sermon about their "defensive humor masking the depth of your personal pain," as if that were necessarily a bad or wrong thing.

Of course, Martin Wagner would be disgusted with them both and write out a fifteen-paragraph email of excoriation telling them why.

Disliking Martin is also part of their bond, although they have a subtle difference in perception of him. Gary thinks Martin ultimately cannot create an identity or life for himself because he so clings to his role of victim. Jonathan believes Martin would have turned out to be an asshole no matter what happened in his life, but being a victim gives him a perfect cover for being so.

They realized, however, once each knew the other's story so thoroughly and well, that to maintain a genuine friendship, they needed something more involving than disliking Martin and rehashing the past, even if it was the past of the previous Tuesday's group. They also recognized the need to escape from being "survivors" and to just enjoy their time together. So, besides dinner, they now go to movies, participate in a monthly amateurs' bowling league, and shop for used books and athletic shoes.

They even tried out a shooting range for a few weeks, an experiment on whether the firing of guns would bring satisfying release from stress, and maybe even from some of the ghosts of their scarring pasts. But it did not. Gary kept losing his footing in the recoil and suffered lingering vibrating torment in his shoulder and arm. Jonathan, who wanted to overcome what he considered an overwrought dread of guns, was appalled by how quickly and easily he took to it, hitting bullseyes more than half the time. It did not stir anger in him or a greater thirst for revenge, but something else. Something he felt more as a ridiculous childish tantrum, a feeling he had indulged too much in his life already. Jonathan worried that shooting guns could sneakily become another addiction or, more accurately, another illusory substitute for the authentic power and control in his life he craved. Guns were removed from their list of options for Thursday evening activities.

The bombastic baritone of Zeke Landers snaps Jonathan back to attention in the present. "I've been pondering the last couple of months that perhaps it is time for me to conclude my involvement with Dr. Birnbaum's Tuesday Evening Therapy Group for Adult Male Survivors of Incest and Childhood and Adolescent Sexual Abuse," he announces with a sweeping dramatic flourish.

His broadcast achieves the desired effect of stunned silence and total attention upon himself. Despite, and often sometimes because of, his grand theatrical affectations, Jonathan enjoys the heavyset, trim-bearded Zeke. At times he could be unusually discerning and sensitive in his reflections on himself and other group members.

"Does...lea-leav-leaving the group...mean you would...al-also stop indi-individ-ual therapy...with Dr. M?" a seriously upset and shaken Paul stammers out with more difficulty than ever.

"Because I don't think you're ready for that at all," Martin hisses with snakelike contempt. His delivery would be hilarious over-the-top camp if not for the fact of it being so smugly hateful.

"In my case, yes. It would." The usually self-dramatizing, round-toned Zeke is now an unperturbed Buddha—one who takes compassionate notice of the sad electric-haired Martin but whose self-possession will not be disrupted by him. An oft-cast supernumerary in the city's major opera company, Zeke had (in his passionate recitals) a once-in-a-lifetime sexual love affair with his vocal coach at age sixteen. Ever since it ended with the coach's arrest and imprisonment for the same crime with another boy, he has failed to find such passion again. Martin has often asserted his moral offense with Zeke's confession that he was relieved his relationship with the coach had never been discovered, allowing him to avoid ever testifying against him.

Before they can absorb Zeke's unexpected news, Gary excitedly proclaims, "I've been thinking the same thing too." He fixes his bright amused green eyes onto Jonathan, telepathically daring him to sing along with this expanding chorus declaring independence.

"Neither of you is in any way, shape, or form capable of being on your own without this group. You haven't dealt with a fraction of what you've been through," Martin pronounces clearly, coldly. He has reached the point where he now sounds so much like a villain in a children's cartoon show that Jonathan literally bites his tongue so he will not burst out laughing.

"I think," intones Bernard Freeman, the only person of color among them, "that both Zeke and Gary display enormous capability in their lives. They prove that in their careers and their ever-improving relationships. Still, what they've endured is immense and profound." He gazes upon the two and candidly addresses them. "I do worry that you carry so much...well, there is no other word, is there? Pain." He briefly stops his measured, thoughtful speech with a nod of his shiny bald head to Martin. "I'm sure that is what he is trying to express in his own way. As am I. Our concern for you."

The velvet-voiced Bernard, a poet with a small cult following and a popular lecturer at local colleges, is without pretension as he shares his words. He has been generous to acknowledge Martin, providing him with some cover of good intention. For reasons unknown, this act touches Jonathan immensely and momentarily loosens the grip of antipathy toward his nemesis.

"Oh, I know I still need a lot of help," Gary chuckles. "I've been researching other therapists and psychiatrists for some time now."

"Splendid!" the grandiloquent Zeke declaims, now directing his eyes on him. Then he adds conspiratorially in his rich, booming voice, "So have I. We must compare notes as to whom we have discovered."

"Yes, I would like to do that," says Gary. "In part to see if you have found someone I haven't who might be a good fit for me but also to be sure we don't end up with the same person or in the same group. Nothing personal," he adds.

"Nothing personal taken." Zeke's Zen composure is unshakable. "I quite understand. It is best for both of us to begin anew without any history or preconceived notions of the members of our new group."

This never-before-seen quality of peaceful equanimity in all things is quite a surprise to the group and perhaps even to Zeke himself. Jonathan considers that Dr. M might deserve some credit for this. Maybe she has been a crucial, life-changing help for Zeke.

"There are a couple of women on my list, which I think is important for me." Gary, more relaxed in the group than Jonathan can ever remember, respectfully directs this remark to the still somewhat deflated and shaken Dr. M, inviting her back into the conversation.

"Well, I'm fucking out," Matt declares. The whole swing of attention by the group to the loss of Zeke and Gary and the abandonment of focus on his heartbreak over losing Amy cements his determination to be free of them all.

"I hope you will stay," Bernard speaks graciously to him. "I think you are a wonderful addition to our group. While your perspective that the spankings you received from your father are not the cause of your depression may well be correct, I wonder if they still had some wounding impact on you that should be explored. I know one pays a price for not examining extraordinary things that have been accepted for many years as ordinary fact."

Insulted for Matt, Jonathan feels the desire rising inside himself to speak on his behalf. He rejects the forty-something poet's sympathetic but false equation of their two records of abuse as somehow sharing a similar, if not the exact same, underlying trauma. It's proof of Matt's point that they do not listen to him. For while Matt's naked spankings seem wrong to Jonathan, he takes his word that those two quick beltings did not shape his relationships with either his father or with Amy or any other path of his life. Bernard's young life as, by his own definition, "a toy" for every male relative, schoolmate, teacher, pastor, church choir member, and white employer in his vanishing Louisiana township was of a different nature altogether. The pasts and presents, and no doubt futures, of Matt and Bernard were vastly different. It seemed not only dishonest and unfair to lock Matt's with Bernard's, it felt imprisoning.

Lost in the labyrinth of his thoughts, Jonathan's eyes unwittingly veer in the direction of Dr. M herself. Jonathan is jarred out of his reverie as he registers that she is observing him. Perhaps for longer than he has been aware. Her usual indefatigable beaming has dimmed somewhat, but she still manages to give him a wan half-smile. She does not avert her eyes from his; indeed, he acutely feels as if he is being scrutinized. He glances away, fast and nervous, disappointed and mad at himself for doing so.

He had once liked Dr. Miriam Birnbaum so very much. The initial blast of her forthrightness and positivity—her easy smile, the constant and steadying encouragement, her absolute faith in his ability to remain sober and drug-free after his ninety-day stint in an expensive private rehab center—were long-thirsted maternal balms. Her unwavering kindness and guidance had been vital in his confronting the years of cruel verbal humiliations that had been his mother's specialty, those embroidered criticisms and judgments that always sought to re-create in him her own misery and self-loathing.

And there was one gift Dr. M had given that he could not deny, and for which he would always be grateful: she had given him permission for often enjoying, even excitedly anticipating, the sporadic sexual acts between his father and himself that had begun at fifteen—a consuming, confusing guilt that had nearly propelled him to suicide.

"You were parched," she explained as he sobbed hysterically in guilt after admitting it aloud, "for affection, affirmation, and touch. This was the one place where you could find it at that time in your life. Warped as the context was, the touch and warmth of skin-to-skin contact was real. So, you experienced the affection and affirmation as real too. Why wouldn't you want to have more of this if it was the only way you thought you could receive it?" Dr. Miriam

Birnbaum's acceptance of this fact, and her prompting of him to accept it, had brought a peace he never imagined possible.

But for several months now, Jonathan has found himself wary of Dr. M. Her Earth Mother persona was wearing thin; he sensed a certain calculation behind it from which she drew power as the one who knew what was needed, what was best and right for them all, that kept them all looking up to her. Verifiable "progress" of some kind could be pointed out in most all their lives—Jonathan himself was in the midst of a career resurgence, building a burgeoning clientele as an extremely popular and highly paid personal trainer at an exclusive gym owned and run by a transman committed, as he phrases it, "to maximizing spiritual healing through holistic body health." But it was just as true that they remained in an unrelieved loop retelling old stories and arguing the same fights, still bound in intricate emotional knots that were not being loosened but, instead, seemed to become more and more inescapable. Jonathan had begun to intuit an invisible contract, known by all but admitted by none, that to be part of this group meant to be eternally bound and in need of her perpetual care. It felt as if they were there to play their parts forever, so Dr. M could likewise play hers.

It seems as if everyone is gabbling and jabbering at once—those leaving the group, those who will never leave, those staying who think it may be right for those who want to leave the group to do so, those who think it is wrong for any of them to change anything at all.

"Our time is running out for tonight," says Dr. M, marshalling her inner forces to impose that absolute boundary from which she will never be dissuaded. "We have a lot to reflect upon and consider. I know a lot of enormously powerful and tumultuous emotions, a tsunami of emotions if you will, has been conjured tonight. Mine most certainly have." She takes a long breath before barreling forward, holding back tears with a mighty effort. "I need to take some time to sit with them before I can articulate exactly what I am thinking and feeling. I just ask that no one make any final decisions about their leaving until we at least speak one-on-one in our individual session." She takes another long deep breath and then asserts with strength, "I hope my boys know that I'm here for them in any way that I can be of service."

"For the fiftieth fucking time, we are not 'your' boys. We belong to ourselves," states adamant, unrelenting Matt.

"You're an asshole," equally adamant, unrelenting Martin shrieks, high and whiney.

And then they are off, and it starts all over again.

"Why can't I talk about Amy?"

"Pl-plea-please don't fi-fight."

"I believe, my friends, we can conduct ourselves with more grace and dignity than this."

"This is sort of why I think it's best for me to leave and start again somewhere else."

"We are your friends and support you in any decision you make. Just don't ignore your longstanding pain."

"Boys. Boys. Our session has ended."

"Goddammit. We are men."

"Don't speak to her that way. Don't speak to any of us that way."

"We sho-should be…ki-kind-kind-er than this."

"Our sensitive friend is most correct. Where are our better angels? These are not our best selves."

"I'm starting to think they are."

"Everyone. Stop. Now. Breathe."

"I loved her."

"I am a victim. You are a victim. We are all victims."

"I wish I cou-could be…clo-clo-close to someone."

"He loved me, and I will always love him."

"I want to be a good husband to my wife and a good father to my child."

"It is only through poetry that I've ever found release from the pain."

"Naked spankings."

"Naked whippings."

"Father."

"Mother."

"Pro-protect…Mo-Mo-Mother."

"Cousins."

"Priest."

"Coach."

"Boss."

"Step-step-fa-father."

"Anybody."

"Everybody."

"Touch."

"Rape."

"Love."

"Abuse."

"Incest."

"Secrets."

"Hide."

"Expose."

"Victims."

"Survivors."

The ceaseless, surreal cacophony of their voices and lamentations suffocate Jonathan with a pity for every one of them. Even for Martin Wagner. But he is also infuriated. He will not, they will not, somehow, impossibly, be made once again innocent and untouched. The unmovable mountain of the past will shadow them all forever.

It is no one's fault, not even Dr. Miriam Birnbaum's. But drowning in this circle of hell known as the Tuesday Evening Therapy Group for Adult Male Survivors of Childhood and Adolescent Incest and Sexual Abuse, Jonathan feels maddened, hurtling toward a place of staggering violence waiting, ready, to be unleashed. And for this, he does blame *them*. It is all *their* fault that he feels this devouring eternal rage.

*Fuck you, Dr. M. Fuck you, Martin. Fuck you, Matt. Fuck you, fuck you, fuck you, Zeke and Bernard and you too, Paul. Fuck you. And even you, Gary. Yeah. Fuck you, too. All of you. Fuck you all,* Jonathan shouts silently within his mind.

But in the swift hot intake of shocked breaths and the Olympic-worthy precision of all heads turning in perfect synchronicity upon him—their eyes reflecting surprise, fear, confusion, and in the case of Gary Leavitt, curious bemusement—awareness gradually dawns over Jonathan Lake. The awareness that after many long mute weeks holding back every thought and every feeling, he has at last spoken up, spoken out. Has finally made his voice heard, himself known.

# Mr. Sissy in Sin City

Mr. Sissy realized he had seen the young man naked earlier that afternoon.

He had been in the hotel's spa, a faux bathhouse modeled on those of ancient Rome, when the young man and his equally young group of male friends entered en masse, all easily naked and jostling each other, loudly invading the quiet with their talk and laughter. Too much physical beauty and over-charged erotic energy so suddenly present. Mr. Sissy's rest and calm had been shattered.

Now the young man was sitting next to Mr. Sissy at the roulette table, perhaps a bit inebriated, reddish hair thick and tousled, grinning wickedly, yet at the same time without guile, his green eyes bright with delight.

*This is truly a happy young man*, Mr. Sissy thought.

And he had to laugh at the young man's snug white t-shirt with big blue letters unapologetically stating, "BAD CHOICES MAKE GOOD STORIES." *English major*, Mr. Sissy surmised, *or perhaps Philosophy. Or just a drunk frat boy proud of his idiocy.* That possibility chilled Mr. Sissy's enjoyment for a moment.

The tall, thin, aging dealer with sunken dark eyes and an elongated face lined with deep creases asked the young man for his ID.

"I'm twenty-one. Today!" he exulted to the dealer. "Finally, legal," he said to Mr. Sissy with a wink.

Mr. Sissy held his frozen half-smile of bemused indifference even as he reeled inside, flush with thrill and nervousness. *Had the young man actually winked at him?*

"Happy birthday," said Mr. Sissy.

"Hey. My name is Michael," the young man said back, extending his strong, muscled arm toward Mr. Sissy for a handshake.

"Hello," Mr. Sissy said, trying to casually match the handshake's strength. "I'm John."

Since no last name had been given by Michael, Mr. Sissy felt no need to give his own—Siskiyou—much less the long family story of how he became nicknamed and forever known, even to himself, as Mr. Sissy.

Still, Mr. Sissy thought, seeing how he would react to the nickname might reveal how comfortably Mr. Sissy could relax and be himself in his presence.

"So how does it work?" asked Michael, loud and over-enthusiastic, as the dealer handed back his ID.

"You've never played roulette?" Mr. Sissy asked.

"Nope. Never. Nada. No way." He laughed, amused at himself and perhaps drunker than he first appeared.

Mr. Sissy placed a ten-dollar chip on the black.

"My boys pussied out," Michael continued, offering an answer to an unasked question. Then he looked startled, sat straight up, and searched the near-empty casino floor. He lowered his voice but kept the celebratory drunken demeanor. "It's only three o'clock, and they couldn't keep it up."

Mr. Sissy registered that Michael was a "man" in legal terms only. But flashing momentarily onto the image his eyes had captured earlier that afternoon in the spa, he mused that the naked body he had observed there—pale white skin and long, naturally muscled frame, leaning back in the warm pool exposing a short and very thick uncut cock—was certainly not that of a boy.

Michael kept talking as Mr. Sissy absently slid two ten-dollar chips on the black, his previous bet having failed. "My boys are great," he spoke fast and eagerly without taking a breath. "But we've been talking about Vegas forever. I'm the last of us to turn twenty-one, and tonight was supposed to be all-out epic. We were going to keep going and going and going until sunrise. The plan was to end up at the fountains...you know, the ones at the Bellagio. But they got too stupid drunk."

He stopped, modestly belched with mustered decorum, then grinned a naive, sweet, yet still somewhat devilish grin. Mr. Sissy could not help but grin back. Michael was definitely attractive, but more importantly to Mr. Sissy, he sensed some basic good-heartedness about the boy-man—some unfettered decency within him no matter how stupid drunk, or troublemaking, he might get.

"Hey! You won!" Michael excitedly proclaimed as he saw the roulette dealer crowning two chips atop Mr. Sissy's bet.

Mr. Sissy lifted the chips between his right thumb and forefinger, then placed them on the square marked EVEN. "You see the last ten numbers have all been odd ones," he explained, pointing to the slim vertical board digitally listing the last ten numbers where the silver ball had dropped. "Now it's more likely to land on an even number sooner rather than later."

"Aaahhhhhhh," Michael slowly exhaled as if coming to some great understanding.

"Playing the odds in a manner of speaking. It's still a matter of luck and chance. It always is," Mr. Sissy emphasized. He became curiously serious, wanting to ensure the young man grasped the essential point. "Always remember that whatever the game you play or how much you bet. You can play smart and strategic with a recognition of the odds. But, ultimately, it always, always, comes down to luck and chance."

There was a pause as Michael frowned with the effort of attempted concentration. He was seriously trying to follow what Mr. Sissy was saying.

Amused and even touched, Mr. Sissy found himself unexpectedly urgent and insistent. "Never ever think for an instant that there's a fool-proof way to beat the house."

"Gotcha!" Michael nodded intently, looking at the board with the numbers lit up, then turning his gaze to the table where the four ten-dollar chips had been laid, and finally back to Mr. Sissy. His green eyes became more vivid, startled even, as if suddenly aware that Mr. Sissy's face had distinct features. The young man was alert and sober now. "Hey! You're the old guy from the spa!"

"Yep, that's me. The old guy," Mr. Sissy acknowledged, knowing he had not suppressed his instinctive wincing at the phrase "old guy." He hoped he recovered his good humor quick enough so that no awkwardness would linger between them. And it was disconcerting, Mr. Sissy now realized, that the young man had seen *him* naked earlier that afternoon. Fat, pasty white, pockmarked, sixty-two-year-old Mr. Sissy with his small, circumcised cock almost hidden by his belly. But before any further conversation could ensue about the sweating steam room of eucalyptus-filtered air or the chilled Arctic room with fake snow, Michael noted that Mr. Sissy had lost his forty dollars on EVEN.

"This is where it gets tricky." Mr. Sissy tried to keep from sounding pedantic. "In order to win back my original forty, I've got to make at least another forty-dollar bet. And, if I really want to come out ahead, I've got to make it at least forty-five. I only have ten-dollar chips, though, so I'm going to have to take a slightly bigger risk and play fifty. Or we could even go higher with sixty." Mr. Sissy immediately caught the "we" and was baffled as to why he included Michael as if they both had a stake in the game.

"That means you would come out...come out...I can't do the math right now for how much ahead you'll be over the forty dollars you've lost." He seemed sincerely sorry he could not be more helpful.

As pleased as he was that Michael was intrigued by the game—and even more pleased that he had something of value to teach him—Mr. Sissy still felt a tinge of embarrassment stab within his chest. He kept returning to images of the young man naked in the warm pool and then later standing under a rushing cascade of cold water in the chilled pool, Michael's back to him, shivering but exhilarated. At the same time, an almost paternal feeling stirred, wanting to guarantee the boy understood the game, so he would not risk all and lose all. Although they had just met, Mr. Sissy wanted to protect him.

"Remember," he spoke patiently, "what I said before. There is absolutely no certainty I will win one-hundred-twenty dollars. None at all. The ball could just as easily land on an odd number again. And then I will have lost sixty. That's a one-hundred-dollar loss in just two plays. That's a lot to lose."

"But all the last numbers have been odd," Michael noted as he glanced again at the digital record of numbers. "I say bet sixty and win a hundred-twenty."

Mr. Sissy chuckled to himself as the old-fashioned phrase "follies of youth" came to mind. "All right," he said, piling ten-dollar chips upon the other.

They sat close to each other in suspenseful silence, watching the roulette dealer place the bullet-small silver ball alongside the polished wood grain and start it on its dizzying spin in the opposite direction of the already rotating wheel. The ball repeatedly rounded the wheel with such stunning velocity it almost seemed like a movie-made special effect.

"YEAAAAHHHH!" Michael exulted without inhibition as the ball finally dropped into the wheel's slot of the even number '20.'

*Good Lord*, Mr. Sissy reflected. *He is so very young.* Of course, except for his ever-dwindling circle of aging friends in Ohio, most everyone was young nowadays to Mr. Sissy.

"See! I told you. I was right. I was right! Sixty was the right amount," Michael almost bellowed, now playfully punching at the side of Mr. Sissy's doughy paunch.

Mr. Sissy jolted out of his reach, happily flushed at the physical attention. "Yes. You were right, and we came out ahead."

"Bet it all on '21.' Bet it all on '21.' Michael was becoming less the young man and more and more a bouncing little boy. "It's my birthday today. I'm twenty-one."

*A boy. A handsome, grinning, red-haired, green-eyed little boy, full of mischief and energy. And a beautiful young man, decent and good-natured, with a naturally muscled body and a short, very thick uncut cock. The son I never had.*

Mr. Sissy intuitively knew the perfect number. "No. Let's bet it on the date. '17.'

"No. '21.' My age."

"No. '17.' Your birth date.

"No. No. Put it on the '21,'" Michael insisted, almost whining. But he did so with such playful bratty exaggeration that Mr. Sissy knew he was saying it more for the fun of the push-pull resistance rather than any serious belief in the magic or rightness of the '21.'

"My money, my bet," Mr. Sissy asserted with deliberate comic and pompous umbrage. He could not believe he was acting so camp with the young man.

"OK, Dad," Michael responded with a long, exaggerated sigh, equally deliberate and comic, the exasperation of a teenage son with his father pulling rank.

Their spontaneous role-play stopped as they both unconsciously held their breath, following the silver ball manically spinning round and round the counter-turning wheel. The ball jumped and tipped and jumped and tipped again, almost settling on various numbers far removed from their choice. And then it stopped for the slightest but most intense cut of time before elegantly sliding down into the '17' slot.

The young man was ecstatic, and Mr. Sissy was swept up as well. His rousing yell of "Yeah!" was every bit as loud and raucous as Michael's.

Without thought, Michael put his arm around Mr. Sissy's shoulder and pulled him close, giving him a long smacking kiss on the right cheek. "Whoa! We got it!" he claimed exuberantly as he broke the embrace and raised his arms triumphantly, fists curled up like a boxer who has just scored the knockout punch.

Mr. Sissy was overwhelmed, disbelieving. The touch of the young man, the strength of his arm around him. The force of being pulled against his beer-and-sweat-scented body. The cheek kiss hot with pleasurable bristles of hair touching Mr. Sissy's face. That quick high wave of maleness—erotic yet unaware of its eroticism—was spellbinding, even as it unsteadied him. Such physical displays with other men that could be witnessed in public simply did not occur in Mr. Sissy's life, especially with a man as young and sexy as Michael.

For the briefest of seconds, they looked directly into each other's eyes, silent. Mr. Sissy's heart beat at such a pounding rate he wondered for a moment if he would suffer the second such attack in his life.

"Gentlemen." The bored, disinterested roulette dealer who had seen it all and heard it all was now speaking. They turned to face him; he, in turn, indicated the stack of chips on '17' to be claimed.

"Oh, yes...yes," Mr. Sissy mumbled as he swept them all toward himself.

"Wow! How much is that?" the awestruck Michael queried.

"Over four thousand dollars," noted Mr. Sissy, regaining his composure but still feeling the hot pulsing rush of the win, the hug, the kiss on the cheek. He separated four one-hundred-dollar chips from the pile and gave them to the dealer. "For you," he nodded. He leaned in conspiratorially with Michael and whispered, "Always tip the dealer after a big win," their heads almost touching.

"But that was four-hundred dollars!" declared Michael.

"And I still have three-thousand-eight-hundred dollars left. You show some class when you share the wealth." Mr. Sissy moved out of their huddle.

Some little spark of appreciation seemed to light the young man's face as he nodded in agreement. Mr. Sissy wondered if Michael could be learning something worthwhile from him. Something about how to act as a man in the world.

"Would you like a drink? After all, you are twenty-one today." Mr. Sissy motioned with a raised hand to attract the attention of a middle-aged cocktail waitress in a too tight, too short, black ruffled skirt roaming nearby on the practically vacant casino floor.

"Yeah. That sounds good," replied Michael, giving Mr. Sissy another conspiratorial wink.

The waitress arrived at the roulette table. She was at the far end of middle age; her face caked with a base of heavy skin-toned makeup. A slash of scarlet lipstick circled her mouth, and her eyelashes were lavishly extended with the aid of long black false ones. It was apparent she was as bored and disinterested with her job as the roulette dealer was with his.

"A Corona, please," Mr. Sissy ordered despite his desire for a way-past-midnight Scotch or Manhattan. "Ice cold with a lime, thank you," he added.

"A Corona, please. Ice cold with a lime, thank you," Michael repeated in perfect and respectful imitation.

Mr. Sissy was relieved by this confirmation that the choice of beer, rather than his usual scotch, better fit Michael's experience with alcohol. "So, how much do you have to play with?" he inquired, shutting back a desire to stupidly giggle at his unintended double entendre.

"I don't have much, but I might be able to stay in for a few rounds."

Mr. Sissy was relieved Michael had no awareness of double entendres. It made him feel better about him for some reason. "Do you have at least fifty dollars?" Mr. Sissy tipped the waitress with two twenties as she served the perspiring long-necked bottles of beer, an extravagant gesture he was shamefully aware he was doing more to impress Michael than express generosity or sympathy for her.

"Yeah, I think so," he said doubtfully. He dug into his pocket and pulled out a small, crumpled wad of bills that he began to count.

"The advantage of playing this early in the morning, besides the table being less crowded, is that the limits are lower. Buy yourself five-dollar chips. Ten of them. That way you can build up your bank."

"My bank?"

"Yes. How much money you have to play with."

And so, for the next hour, Mr. Sissy was in his element as teacher. He defined the inside and outside of the table layout for the young man and the payoff odds that depended on where the bet was placed. He shared his own minor strategies and superstitions developed over years of Las Vegas vacations, such as putting down only modest single bets at first. That way, Michael could avoid depleting his original bank too early and fast and, ideally, have a better chance of incrementally increasing his amounts to bet.

Michael was a fast student as he picked up the different ways to play the table. He paid careful heed to the pole displaying the previous numbers hit, noting whether they were odd or even or red or black. He also understood the importance how the numbers correlated with the columns on the table, as well as how they were divided on the outside border, calculating the impact every placement could have on his potential winnings. He seemed to thrive on the attention Mr. Sissy gave him. There was no longer any loud, drunken bravado but instead, a studious, unaffected earnestness to play and master the game despite Mr. Sissy's repeated reminders that ultimately there was no way to master luck itself.

Mr. Sissy could not help himself. He felt a swell of tenderness for Michael, sensing that perhaps he was lonely, disappointed that his friends had abandoned him in his big adventure of turning twenty-one in Sin City. Maybe he had felt lonely even when he was naked and jostling with his equally naked and jostling young friends earlier in the spa. Mr. Sissy remembered a truth that he too often forgot now that he was older and no longer taught as a profession: most boys, young men, even the handsome ones, naked and smooth white, naturally muscled with uncut thick cocks—even *them*—could feel so powerfully lonely at times, even lost.

And he knew that whatever their age or sexuality, most males in their loneliness had a hungry need for nothing more than spending time in the uncomplicated, undemanding company of another male.

The faces and bodies and times spent with other young men, times when Mr. Sissy himself was a young man, began to swim up in his memories. And recent memories as well. Particularly those of a disastrous relationship with someone nearly thirty years younger than he. And the brief period afterward where Mr. Sissy paid for the faces and bodies of even younger men to spend time with him. But he would not dwell. Instead, he reminded himself of the promise he made when turning sixty—Mr. Sissy would not allow Act III of his life to be spent in regret over faces and bodies, either in decades past or of recent years. He accepted his romantic and sexual life as it had occurred, and he would not waste his remaining time in shame or regret over any of it.

He sighed a private sigh and redoubled his focus on Michael, pointing out things about his bets, teasing him gently and without agenda. He could feel the boy's loosening of intensity and push as he became more absorbed by the game, more at ease in being himself. They played a while longer, winning, losing, regaining, getting ahead, losing, winning. All the cycles of the game. But Michael stayed in and nearly doubled his money.

Eventually, the dealer announced he was closing the table. If they wanted to continue playing, he directed, they could move to the roulette table at the other end of the essentially deserted casino. There were no more than a dozen players remaining among the game tables or slots. Despite the beeps, clangs, and bings of the multitude of colorfully lit machines and the never-ending piped-in pop music of the 1980s, an undercurrent of quiet had enveloped the enormous room.

Mr. Sissy and the young man sat, tired and comfortable, silent in their thoughts, nursing their third round of beers after the dealer had left.

Slowly, imperceptibly, as their silence drew out, Michael's body moved closer and closer toward Mr. Sissy's, subtly leaning in, until finally, effortlessly, in the grace of a natural dance, his head fell lightly upon Mr. Sissy's shoulder. Once again, Mr. Sissy took in the sensual beer-and-sweat scent of the young man's strong body, hard muscled but soft and pale-skinned. To be so close to him like this was a blessing that gave his spirit peace.

Michael sighed loud and contentedly, his head almost nuzzling against Mr. Sissy's shoulder and neck.

Mr. Sissy fought the urge to put his arm around him and bring the young man in even closer and tighter. He was filled with a fierce desire, a fierce need, to keep him safe from all he knew the world would do to him as he moved onward into his adulthood.

At one point, apropos of nothing, Michael spoke. "I'm sorry we made so much noise in the spa."

His sincerity pierced Mr. Sissy deeply. *He is a good boy. Good in the truest and best old-fashioned meaning of the word. This son I never had.*

"Oh, that's alright," Mr. Sissy assured him.

"We were being assholes. I could see we were disturbing you."

Mr. Sissy gulped for air, then spoke low and soft, even though no one was remotely near them. "You weren't being assholes. Well, maybe you were." But he made this comment with a teasing chuckle that made Michael smile and put him even more at ease. "You were all just having a good time. It's what you're supposed to do at twenty-one." Mr. Sissy prevented himself from saying anything further or making an unnecessary joke, his habitual defaults whenever he started to feel the genuine weight of caring for another.

"I saw you sneaking peeks at us," Michael said, matter-of-factly and without admonishment.

Mr. Sissy's heart began to pound hard and crazy again. For a moment or two, he could not even breathe. He felt the spinning dizziness in his brain, his thoughts like the silver metal ball whirling madly around the roulette wheel.

With a quick breath, he stammered, "I'm sorry."

"Oh, no big deal." Michael sat up straight, arching his back and raising his arms in a long unbroken stretch, accompanied by an equally long unbroken yawn. "I like being looked at." His head fell back onto Mr. Sissy's shoulder, cozy and affectionate.

Though he still could not properly, fully breathe, Mr. Sissy's mind rushed through his long-held but now deeply buried fantasies of love and romance. He knew young men nowadays were far more vocal and honest in stating their sexual interests and longings, having seen in personal ads online the acknowledgment, without hesitancy or explanation, of lusts and fetishes, and even desired relationships with older men, fat men, feminine men. Men like Mr. Sissy. Could Michael possibly be one of those young men who placed such ads?

The young man puppishly snuggled beside him, his eyes closed, Mr. Sissy glanced down at the roulette table. He weighed what words to say, what action to take. Should he propose they go to the Bellagio fountains? Should he ask him up to his room to be held close, like now, as they slept? And hope the connection between them could hold after they woke?

"You've been very nice to me tonight," Michael finally spoke.

"I'm happy to have met you."

"You know, it was turning out to be a real suck of a birthday. I know they didn't mean to fuck it up, but I was pretty pissed off when my guys gave up and went back to our room."

"Well, that's certainly understandable."

"But you made my night. I learned the game. Won some money. Shared some drinks. Had a lot more fun than I thought I would."

"And it's been a real pleasure for me to spend time with you, Michael."

"You're a good guy. Easy to be around. I don't usually hang with older guys, so this has been different. But I've enjoyed myself."

"Thank you."

Michael took in and then exhaled a long, deep breath. "You know, if I was into gay stuff, I would let you blow me," he said in a whisper, looking around to see if anyone was near them.

Unexpectedly, now that the sexual current was acknowledged and in the open, Mr. Sissy almost laughed out loud at Michael's blunt admission. But, of course, he did not. He knew in his own way the young man was risking himself. In his own way, he was saying something private only to Mr. Sissy. It should not be laughed at.

Michael kept talking. "I once let this guy in my dorm freshman year suck me off. And a couple of times me and one of my boys jerked off together." He hesitated, gathering his feelings. "But it just wasn't for me, you know?" He lifted his head off Mr. Sissy's shoulder. He looked at him, his green eyes almost imploring. "I'm really sorry."

"Stop," said Mr. Sissy, placing his hand upon the boy's shoulder without even being aware he was doing so. "You don't have anything to be sorry for. Never ever apologize for being who you are."

*Keep him safe, God. Please keep this beautiful son I never had safe.*

"Happy birthday," Mr. Sissy spoke, sharply feeling regret in knowing he would never see Michael again.

Then he slid all his remaining gold chips toward him. He stood up to leave. "A birthday present. Every young man should have some extra cash in his pocket for his first trip to Vegas."

Michael's brilliant green eyes went wide with astonishment as he stared at the columns of chips now in front of him. He grinned his goofy, mischievous grin at Mr. Sissy. "No, I can't. It's way too much."

Mr. Sissy looked him directly in the eye. His voice was suddenly emotional with a barely discernible but still potent shaking. "You must. It's my birthday gift to you."

"Are you sure?" Michael, still disbelieving, asked with a twinge of some emotion in his voice as well.

Mr. Sissy rallied. His voice was gentle but assured. Again, he deliberately looked at Michael directly. "Absolutely! Live it up! Bet it all on '21' if you want," he said with a wink. "Or show your friends there's no bad feelings. Take them out to dinner at an expensive restaurant. Treat them to a show."

Michael's smile had returned, but he could only repeat, "Are you sure?" as his voice shifted into a higher pitch.

Mr. Sissy smiled a big, joyous smile. "Just promise that someday when you're an old fat man with gray hair you'll do something nice for a young man celebrating his twenty-first birthday. Maybe your son. OK?"

"OK," Michael said. Then, he shyly asked, "Are you sure you don't want to play some more?"

Mr. Sissy again weighed the possibility of proposing they go to the Bellagio fountains. He knew outside it had to be nearing sunrise. Perhaps breakfast, if not bed? But he shook his head in a 'No' instead. He gave Michael a wave goodbye and turned away from him and the table, making a slow, proud exit, unhurried and measured in his pace.

For Mr. Sissy knew the most important lesson of gambling and, indeed, life itself. Something Michael could only learn in the passage of years through love risked, love won, and love lost: that one must trust when to walk away, having won enough.

# The Barbies in the Closet

Even though he was eight years old and knew the difference between real and pretend, he was afraid of the Barbies in the closet once he was in bed and the room was all dark. He knew they were in there whispering, saying mean things about him, making fun of him. They called him "sissy," and "queer," and "weakling," and other names despite being his best friends during the daytime. He knew they wanted to do bad things to him.

*Bitches!*

He didn't know exactly what that word meant, but he knew it was a bad word. It was a word that would get him in trouble if Mama heard him say it out loud, even though he had learned it from her. She said it when she talked about the other mothers in their building who looked down on her like she was no good. The Barbies acted the same way toward him once they were by themselves in the closet.

He could never figure out why the Barbies—so beautiful and so much fun to play with and dress up in the gowns he drew, and that Mama made real on her sewing machine—would turn against him at night. Then, during the day, when it was bright and sunny, they would play together with the Barbies acting out stories he made up for them. Exciting romantic stories where they traveled to faraway places like Paris and Rome that he saw in old movies on their black-and-white TV set with the rabbit ears. The ones starring glamorous women, magical women, like Audrey Hepburn and Ann-Margret. The Barbies were so famous and adored in these places they did not need a last name. He was often with them in these stories, and there everyone knew him by one name too—

Dayday, Mama's name for him instead of "David," which she only called him when she was mad.

The Barbies were being especially bad tonight. He couldn't sleep because he just knew that all four of them were inside the closet that faced his bed, talking about him among themselves, pointing at him, then giggling just like all the different groups of kids did in his third-grade classroom—the popular and pretty ones, the rich ones, and the super-smart and the super-dumb ones, even the ones nobody else liked.

He knew how much trouble he would get into if he got caught out of bed this late at night. If Mama came in, she would grab him roughly by the arm, digging her sharp pointy fingernails deep into it, almost picking him up as she dragged him back to bed, and giving him fast, hard smacks on the bottom. His hand-me-down pajamas with Roy Rogers riding his palomino horse Trigger on them were really thin and worn-out, so those smacks would hurt. But he wanted to catch the Barbies in the closet huddled together, talking about him, thinking up things to do to him that would hurt his feelings and maybe even his body. He would prove to them he wasn't fooled at all when they pretended to like him in the daytime.

He knew he had to be very, very sneaky and quiet so the bedsprings wouldn't make too much noise and wake up Mama. He held his breath as he slowly sat upright, pulling back the blue-and-red-checkered blanket. Then he turned to sit on the side of the bed. He was very still, making sure he didn't breathe loudly. With a very fast but silent-as-a-mouse movement, he stood up. For a few seconds, he was like a statue. He tried not to breathe, being sure Mama was still asleep. He could feel his heart beating fast.

Once he knew she had not woken up, he walked to the closet on his tiptoes like a ballerina. He was positive he could hear the whispers of the chattering Barbies behind the door. They were mocking his own girlish voice just like so many of the boys did at recess during the daily soccer game they were all forced to play by Sister Francis Theodora, the old nun who looked like a scarecrow. She always kept the boys and girls far apart on the playground.

The closet had a glass doorknob that he sometimes pretended was a big diamond that opened a gateway to a more colorful, magical world, like when Dorothy opens the door of her house after the tornado and walks out to the wonderful world of Oz. A light bulb came on inside the closet without him having to pull a string or flip a switch, which added to the dizzy sense of a hidden world suddenly appearing. He began to turn the diamond knob with great concentration so no noise would be made. He held his breath again as he turned the knob as slowly as he could, his hands gripped tight around it.

Then he made the quick, dramatic gesture of opening the door wide. Not daring to speak out loud, he said, "Aha!" in his mind. He was positive the Barbies could hear him.

But looking down to the floor of the closet, he saw they had been able to turn back into their usual Barbie selves right at the moment he opened the door and the light came on.

They stood up against the ugly, dark, black wood box, filled with his other toys—bright, colorful building blocks and small green plastic army soldiers and cowboys riding horses. All kinds of balls in every sort of shape and size. And the games that he had outgrown, like Uncle Wiggily and Candyland. The Barbies were dressed up in his sophisticated creations. He didn't know exactly what "sophisticated" meant either, but Mama had used the word when she saw his drawings for the dresses, and he knew it was a very important compliment because of the way she said it. He liked the way the word sounded. "Sophisticated" had to be something grown-up and rich and classy, he just knew.

One of the Barbies wore a shiny long gold gown with matching long gold gloves that went up past her elbows. Another had on a sleeveless, low-cut red velvet top with a blue belt cinching a big wide white skirt at the waist. ("Cinching" was a sewing word he had learned from Mama that he always made the effort to use correctly.) The third Barbie wore a tight body-hugging full-length glittery black dress with lacy black sleeves and a wide lace train running many inches behind her. And the fourth and last Barbie was wearing the best gown of them all—a bright pink balloon dress trimmed with white fur over the edges of an open slit that went down the front, almost to her belly button.

Mama had made sure that what she called the "plunging neckline" still covered Barbie's boobies. "Plunging" was his new favorite word. But he also knew he didn't want his drawings to all look the same, so he had decided to use a "plunging" neckline only once in a while for his gowns. He liked the word "gowns" better than he did "dresses" too. Every woman wore dresses, but only the most gorgeous and glamorous and famous women wore "gowns."

The Barbies were hushed and unmoving in the bright white light. He thought for a moment about what he should do now but could think of nothing. So, he closed the door as noiselessly as possible, going slower and slower, then slower more, keeping his eyes fixed on them all the time until, at last, the light went off, and it was shut. He tiptoed his way back to bed, this time making large, wide steps like he had seen Elmer Fudd do when he went hunting for Bugs Bunny or Daffy Duck. He couldn't explain it, but he always thought Daffy Duck was a lot funnier than Donald Duck.

Back in bed with his blanket over him again, he closed his eyes for sleep.

But it was impossible. He knew that as soon as he shut the door all the way back, the Barbies' small black eyes turned to flames of burning hate. Their pursed little red lips had grown into wicked smiles from which tiny, pointy fangs fell, at first hardly noticeable, but then so sharp that they could cut deep into him with one bite.

He tried so hard to make himself not see the Barbies' faces, not to think about all the horrible things they would do to him if they were set free. He got more and more anxious, more and more frightened. He was convinced that tonight was the night the Barbies in the closet were going to kill him.

He lay in his bed, frozen in terror. The Barbies would wait until he was fast asleep and then sneak out of the closet and climb up his bed. Even when they saw the crucifix of Jesus on the cross above it, next to the taped-up magazine picture of the murdered President Kennedy (who he daydreamed was his real father), they would surround him and eat at his face, tearing it away. They would whisper to him that he was ugly and stupid and a sissy and a girl and a queer. That no one loved him, that everyone hated him. Even Mama since she would sometimes yell at him, "Act like a boy!" whenever he danced around imitating the actresses in the movies. The Barbies would be very happy as they did all these things.

He tried harder and harder to remember that the Barbies were not real and could not do anything bad to him. But some other feeling was stronger tonight, some other sense about them. The Barbies secretly were the devil's girlfriends. They would take him to hell. And once there, they would make him strip off his pajamas and underwear, pointing at his tiny wiener, laughing as nasty as they could. Then they would push him down into a giant pit of hot red and orange hellfire where he would fall and fall and keep falling, never stopping, never landing, never hitting the bottom, just always falling while burning eternally. He knew what "eternally" meant. He shuddered like he was outside in the cold, even as he felt hot and clammy under the blanket.

He had to do something to save himself from the Barbies.

He got out of bed, much less slow and careful this time though still aware of not making a sound that might wake Mama up. He stood for a long time before the closet door, not even touching the knob. He had to think of what he was going to do first. There were no murmurs from the closet, but he knew the

Barbies were aware of him standing on the other side. They were waiting for him to make his next move. He wondered if they were now hiding in different places in the closet, getting ready to jump and attack as soon as he opened the door.

He walked over to his desk in soft steps. On the top of it were his pens and colored pencils and "sketchbook," as Mama had called it. A "sketchbook" meant his drawings were different, important even, something almost adult that he should be proud of even though he never showed it to anyone but her. And even then, he only did so when he sensed she was not in one of her bad moods that seemed to be happening more and more lately.

At first, Mama had been surprised, happy even, at the many dresses he had drawn with so much color and "flair," whatever that word meant. She seemed to look at him with so much pride after going through his drawings. She had been eager to help him make the dresses come to life with her sewing machine. She taught him much about patterns and stitching and all the different kinds of thread and fabrics that could be used.

But something had started to change. She was impatient with him more than usual now. She didn't want to spend as much time looking at what he drew in the sketchbook, and he was hesitant to ask her too often to make his drawings into real gowns. Mama seemed sad and mad sometimes when she looked at him and would go into her room and close the door, angrily telling him to go outside and play with the other boys in the building. But then, a few hours later or the next day or the day after that, like the sun coming out after a long, gray, rainy day, she would open the door and call him in and ask to see his latest work. She even got excited again about something she saw there, wanting to do all the work that had to be done for the Barbies to wear them.

Finally, he found the medium-sized pair of scissors with the big plastic orange handles he was looking for. He also saw the roll of strong white string that he would sometimes tie around his finger so tight it turned the finger blue, leaving a deep dent once he unwrapped it.

He knew if he could get the Barbies all tied up together, they would have no way to get out of the closet for the rest of the night while he slept. So, he cut a long section of the tough string from its roll.

He opened the closet door just a little bit at a time, inch by inch by steady inch, holding his breath longer with each widening of the door, almost more thrilled than he was afraid. He tried to make them out in the dark, spying on them through the slight crack that became larger and larger until the light in the closet came alive and glowed again upon them. The Barbies were standing exactly where they were when he had last seen them a few minutes ago.

His stomach churned and hurt at being called "sissy" by them, the way it felt when kids at school called him that and all the other names. He hated being made fun of—imitated for how he walked or moved his hands—and being whispered about and pointed at, even when he was right there in front of them. It all ran like a hot fever through him, leaving him feeling sick and angry, when he saw the Barbies lined up in the magnificent gowns he had made for them, knowing they were just like everybody else in how they talked about him.

He picked up all four Barbies in one scoop. Then, holding them in his hand, looking at each of their long, smooth plastic faces, he decided they would be the ones forced to be naked. This way, their gowns would not be crushed and wrinkled, and maybe they would be more thankful to him in the morning when he gave them back, and they could be dressed up in them again.

He was very tender with each Barbie as he first removed their shoes, neatly lining them up on top of the toy chest, and then as he unzipped or unfastened or unbuttoned their lovely clothes, pulling them off gently in a gliding motion—like he was stroking them, soothing away all their worries and pains. The way Mama sometimes did when he was sick or after he was punished by her. He placed each outfit right below its matching pair of shoes.

He started to feel ashamed now that the Barbies were naked. Maybe they shouldn't be without the gowns that made them look like movie stars. Maybe he was doing a bad thing. He thought of putting their clothes back on them. But he wondered if he did, and left them alone in the closet, if they would become meaner and madder, carrying out an even bloodier plan to harm him.

How angry and punishing they really were, no matter how much makeup or jewels or furs or specially designed gowns he gave them! The Barbies had so much *power*. He knew they could not be trusted, and he had to do something to protect himself against them.

At first, he couldn't make up his mind if the Barbies should be pressed against each other face-to-face or if it would be nicer and less scary for them if they could look out into the dark, their faces away from each other. That way, while still being close by each other's side, they could still talk but without breathing on each other. Face-to-face, he decided, would be awful if one of them became sick and had to puke. Facing out, they couldn't get sick on each other. That would be the kinder thing to do.

He tied the thin string around them tighter and tighter until there was only enough string left to make a couple of knots that were also extremely tight and impossible to break. He felt like he was a villain on TV, and he enjoyed being the villain with all the power. But it also made him feel guilty and wrong. He was never ever this bad during the daytime at school or in front of Mama.

He wondered if the next time he went to confession at church, he should tell the priest about his sin of taking off all the Barbies' clothes and tying them up naked. He was immediately worried and afraid at what the priest would say and what penance he might give him for this sin. Many months ago, he told the priest about his impure act of putting the eraser end of a pencil into his butt while he rubbed his balls and wiener. The priest had become angry and yelled at him from where he sat alone in his own dark space. He had made him swear at the feet of the Virgin Mary that he would never do such a thing ever again. For his penance, he had to say the rosary every night for a whole week.

But confession would come later. Right now, he leaned the tied-up circle of Barbies against the toy box. Unfortunately, that meant one of them would have to face the box all night and not look out. He promised if he woke up at any point, either from a bad dream or if he had to go pee—both of which happened almost every night—he would be sure to come back and move them around so that each Barbie would share the punishment of facing the toy box. That was fair.

His most secret wish in the world was that maybe a couple of the girls at his school would become his friends and that they could play with their Barbies together. One rainy day when they couldn't go outside to play during recess, Sister Francis Theodora let them either go to the library or stay in the room and talk in clusters. It was the only time she let the boys and girls be next to each other, even though all the girls and all the boys—except him—still stayed apart.

He sat sort of outside the edge of a group of girls, listening as they talked about their Barbies. He was too scared to tell them that he had four Barbies himself and that he drew their dresses and gowns, even though he wanted to so badly. Then, the subject changed to the different boys in their class. Who was cute. Who was nice. Who was nasty. Who was funny. Who was cute.

The girls were surprisingly curious about what he had to say about the other boys, even though he didn't talk at all about their looks or use the word "cute," or even "handsome," to describe them. Somehow, he knew he couldn't do that. They were all whispering and gossiping and laughing among themselves when tall, wrinkled Sister Francis Theodora suddenly appeared, dressed in her black garb like a witch. She stood above them, looking down only at him. She said nothing for what seemed like forever, then spoke in the most hateful tone of voice he had ever heard. In a mocking high-pitched prissy voice not at all like her normal one, she said, "My, what a *darling* little sweetie girl you are."

He felt like he had been stung by a hundred million bees all at once, his face turning hot and red. All the girls in the group laughed, except Mary Lou Johnson, the only Negro girl in the whole school. After Sister Francis Theodora moved on, Mary Lou leaned over to him and whispered, "She's a bitch!" But he never joined their group again during rainy recesses, nor was he ever asked to do so by any one of them, even Mary Lou. He would, instead, go off to the school library and read the books with Greek myths and Indian legends or look at old *Life* magazines with pictures of movie stars like Elizabeth Taylor in *Cleopatra*.

The Barbies were his only friends.

But now he heard it. The whispering again. It was so strange because even though they were not whispering out loud, he could clearly hear them. "We are not going to take this. Not from *him*! Not from *that* little sissy! That little *queer*. He's not going to get by with it. We'll get our revenge! He'll find out exactly what we can do to him!"

"Goddammit! Goddammit! Goddammit!" He wasn't sure if he said the word to himself in his mind or if he said it out loud. Mama never said that word except when she was at her angriest or most tired. He would never ever dare say it out loud to her or anybody. He knew that even saying it in his mind meant that he would have to add it to his list of sins for his next confession. That it might even be worse than tying the Barbies up naked. Or wanting to go swimming naked himself and joined by that boy tied up on the altar by his father in the Bible picture book he got for his first communion.

But he said "Goddammit" to himself again. This time he was sure it was only in his mind, but it felt so good. Even if it was a sin.

He felt cold, sticky sweat across his forehead and underneath his pajama top. His heart was beating incredibly fast and loud again, and he started to feel dizzy.

He hated the Barbies now, and they hated him more than ever before. They were going to hurt him in any awful way they could the next chance they got. They were going to torture him and kill him and drink his red blood and smear it all over their naked bodies. He just *knew*. His hate. Their hate. It all kept building and building. He could feel it all over his body.

No longer thinking about how much noise he was making, he went to his desk and picked up the scissors with the orange handles again, as well as a roll of scotch tape.

He returned to the closet, knowing what he had to do. The first and most important thing was to shut the Barbies up. That was what the scotch tape was for. He took a strip of it off the roll and held it sticking to one of his fingers. Next, he cut teeny-tiny strips with the hand holding the scissors. These teeny-tiny patches would cover the Barbies' mouths and maybe even part of their faces, but they wouldn't be so big as to cover their noses where they couldn't breathe. Nor would they be so long that they would reach the Barbies' ears and mess up their hair.

He had to pay strict attention so he would do it right. He tried many times before he had the exact size of scotch tape to fit over their mouths. In fact, he decided to double-tape them so there would be no way on earth they could be heard. It had been a good idea to have the Barbies facing out when he tied them up earlier, since this made it easier for him to tape over their little lips now without having to untie them. Once their mouths were covered, he held the group in his hand, happy and satisfied at his work.

Then he had his best idea yet. He went to the low-set chest of drawers next to his desk. From the bottom one, where Mama kept his two other sheets and bedding, he removed a light-blue pillowcase.

He was going to be absolutely, totally, positively sure that the Barbies could not talk, could not see, could not be heard, and could not escape. He took the naked group and placed them inside the pillowcase. He twisted it around and around so that he could turn the top into a long line, thick but not very thick. Then he tied it into a knot.

Now that the Barbies were tied up in the blue pillowcase, he let out a long gasp of air, breathing for what seemed to be the first time that whole night. But he was stubbornly determined that the Barbies would never be able to find a way to get out whatsoever. On his knees inside the closet, he slid out three stacks of cardboard shoeboxes, two to each stack, that had been neatly arranged into the left corner—some with shoes, some with toys like marbles and jacks, others empty. Once cleared, he placed the pillowcase of the four tied-up, mouth-taped, naked Barbies in the spot. Then, he took the six shoeboxes and arranged them as a two-sided fort, high and close. It would be impossible for the Barbies to see through or climb over it, even if they found a way to untie themselves and escape out of the blue pillowcase. The Barbies were defeated at last.

He made his way back to his bed, mindful more than ever that there would be an awful punishment if Mama woke up and found him out of it so late in the night. He was as silent as if he was a ghost, barely moving.

Once back in bed, the covers pulled over him, he prayed. "Thank you, God, for keeping me safe from the Barbies. Forgive me for taking off their clothes and tying them up. I promise I will be good to them tomorrow. I'll treat them extra nice and make beautiful new gowns for them."

He closed his eyes, feeling himself easing into sleep at last. He knew there might still be torments and nightmares to come before morning. But at least none of them would be caused by the Barbies in the closet.

*Bitches!*

# Today's Agenda

Professor Edward Duncan, all sixty-nine years and two-hundred-eighty-five pounds of him, sat hunched over the desk in his cluttered office, reading awful student midterm essays with a masochistic despair that had gone on for so many years now he no longer felt energized or engaged by it.

In attempt to awaken his brain from the enveloping stupor caused by relentless bad writing, he would sometimes lean as far back as the creaky old springs of his hard pine wood swivel chair allowed, holding an essay at arm's length. His face moved in contorted patterns of confusion, dismay, and finally, disgust, accompanied by almost operatic cries of mock and not-so-mock anguish. He stopped, took a deep breath, and then energetically attacked the jargon-filled paper, an investigation into every line the n-word appeared in *Kingdom of Earth*—one of the lesser-known plays of Tennessee Williams— purportedly "proving" that the racism expressed within was not of an ignorant, panicked backwater Southern prostitute, but that of Williams himself. With bold, quick strokes of his red pencil, he crossed through lines and lines of text, finishing with plentiful, often sarcastic, commentary in the margins. Each semester students' writing became more abysmal and offensive to him. Professor Edward Duncan had no patience nor pretense left to care how his remarks would be received.

Putting the paper aside, he surveyed the over-stuffed room packed to the ceiling with mountains of books (most of them read), along with administrative and departmental reports, memorandum, and studies (never to be read). Multitudinous, thick files of research materials, some of which dated a decade or longer, and various-sized piles of published, unpublished, and uncompleted plays, manuscripts, and academic articles written by colleagues (some now dead) were strewn all over the floor. Drafts of dissertations by desperate, pleading doctoral students joined the mess. Only two clear, but narrow, pathways existed—one to his desk and one to the beaten, scratched brown leather chair across from it for students and other rare visitors.

His desk was a swamp of more books, literary and academic journals, student papers, and administrative reports. There was also a computer he resented, a faux art deco desk lamp he had salvaged from a thrift store some forty years earlier, and a silver framed photo of Malcolm that he looked at many times a day and three times as often when he graded papers. The joyously smiling face of his long-deceased African American lover, a face that could without hyperbole be properly described as beaming, was his reprieve, his encouragement, and sometimes, in his most despondent and hopeless moments, his prayer.

But the truth was, as Professor Edward Duncan slid more and more thoughtlessly and unhappily into Act III of his life, he had a harder time gazing upon the exuberant, almost beatific Malcolm. Looking at the photo could now ignite reproach, a reminder not only of the loss of his great love but also of all that he has lost of himself, and of what he has become—and what he has not— since Malcolm's death from AIDS nearly thirty years ago.

Two brisk hard knocks at his office door shocked him out of yet another of his frequent driftings. Before he could even utter permission to enter, Professor Shirley Church opened the door. She paused a few moments before walking in. He knew that she purposely stood in the frame, so he could take in her full dramatic portrait—a tall, long-limbed, proudly poised woman he and Malcolm once affectionately teased as "the Amazon." She was dressed in her daily uniform of black buttoned-down long-sleeved men's shirt and form-fitting black slacks, which was usually offset by blazer of primary color (bold yellow, bright red, royal purple) or a tunic of an African tribal print. Today, it was one of her tunics, this one filled with a green-and-orange background and oddly shaped ebony figures and lines and symbols he could not decipher. Except for the graying of her close-cropped tight hair, she was virtually unchanged from the first day they met when he was quite young and she even younger.

"This is your doing," Shirley said, wildly shaking a sheet of paper, which he recognized as the list of items on today's agenda for their Theater Department's monthly faculty meeting.

"Live by the tweet, die by the tweet, Professor Church. That's the way of the world now, isn't it?" He surprised himself and was much pleased by this bit of improvised dialogue. It was the perfect thrust and parry regarding the item he knew she was referring to.

"You're better than this. I take that back. You *were* better than this."

Edward almost smiled. Shirley Church is every bit his match and knows how to improvise dialogue as theatrical as his own. Words truly never fail her.

She strode in, making her way to the tattered chair in front of his desk. Even in this short walk, Professor Duncan was struck by the panther grace of her movement. "It was an opinion," she said. "About a *movie!*"

"Wrong movie to have the wrong opinion about it seems," he archly responded.

Their shared past, especially their shared past with Malcolm, still bound them. They also could amuse each other, though much less often than before, sparking each other's intellect and spirit. But there was no way to deny they had become less tolerant of foibles and flaws they had supposedly accepted long before. Professor Shirley Church has told her most trusted nonwhite colleague within the university that Professor Edward Duncan "works my very last frayed, hanging by a single sliver-thread nerve."

"I know you don't believe this nonsense that's been going around, Eddie." She is one of the half-dozen people in his lifetime who have ever been allowed to name him as such. His mother, his nephew, a once-best friend now suffering from dementia in an assisted living facility, his first lover not seen or heard from in over forty-five years, and of course, Malcolm were the only others.

"Oh, of course I know it's nonsense. And I'm sorry, genuinely sorry, you've been marked, or I guess 'memed' is the word these days, as some sort of traitor to African Americans and feminists."

"But not so sorry you won't use it as advantage." Her dark-brown eyes brimmed with anger.

"Yes. That's true," he said, his milky blue-gray ones bluntly meeting hers. There was no reason to obfuscate at this point.

Shirley stood up from the chair with such swift suppleness it reminded him of a beautiful dancer in flight. She turned her back to him and was silent. He knew her well enough that he should say nothing and just wait. Any further words from him would only provoke her. Suddenly, she pivoted back to face him. "I know you disagree with the policy change, Eddie, but this is an underhanded bullshit way to stop it."

"It's not a policy change yet," he volleyed back, trying to keep his voice modulated, even. "Right now, it's still just a proposal."

Shirley wills her voice not to break. *Don't cry. Don't cry. Don't cry.* That is the mantra she silently repeats to herself. But sadness is flowing into her wrath, and she knows that combination could fill her with the tears she must never let anyone see. Especially any of her colleagues and, most especially, any who are white. Even if it is her once-great friend Professor Eddie Duncan, the widower of her even greater friend Malcolm.

"You used to be my best ally in this minefield," she says.

"You were always so open to learn back then," is his answer. He winces inwardly as soon as he says it, regretting the unintended patronization.

But if what he has said has registered as such, she gives no indication. Instead, she just ruefully notes, "So were you."

◆◆◆

He feels the strong pull toward the comforting territory of memories, to repeated cherished stories of when she first interviewed thirty-five years earlier for the assistant faculty position. He had been Shirley Church's most fervent advocate despite his own relatively low rank at the time, having just won tenure. Fresh from receiving her doctorate, she had only one academic journal publication to her name—a brilliantly researched piece on female African American playwrights of the early twentieth-century Harlem Renaissance, which had been an eye-opener for Eddie about his own lack of knowledge.

Though "multiculturalism" was the buzzword of that era, Malcolm had been the one to make him aware how essential, how vital, it was for both white and minority students to have a Black face to see and, far more importantly, a Black voice to hear. "The faculty too," Malcolm had laconically added.

"It's important the little dumbasses know there's more than Lorraine Hansberry and *A Raisin in the Sun*. And she will bring in new students and new audiences from the community that we have never reached before," Eddie had zealously argued to the hiring committee, quoting Malcolm without attribution.

Shirley quickly proved how right he was on all counts. She knew how to leverage the wattage of her charisma and intelligence—as well as white eagerness to be seen as fair and open-minded. And, most crucially, *cooperative.* She soon had the recently published script of August Wilson's *Fences* placed as assigned reading in not only the general education Introduction to Theater class but also the Introduction to Literature and Introduction to Humanities courses. The baseball-themed play with its father-son dynamic was immensely popular, and instructors across the fields noted that it hooked more male students into discussions about a play than anything they had ever taught of Shakespeare or Moliere or O'Neill. The following academic year, there was a slight but definite uptick of nontheater majors signing up for both dramatic literature and acting classes, including the highest enrollment of African American students majoring in the department than ever before. A grand total of six.

In her second year, Shirley promoted color-blind casting, which was then a "radical" concept for the minor, barely known university in Iowa. She did so not only because she passionately believed it had to be done to give students of color more chances to be cast and gain experience in classical roles, but also because of Malcolm.

He and Eddie were "live-in lovers," as was the popular phrase at the time of Eddie's own hire, having met two years before at their previous university in Michigan. Malcolm, who had parlayed his Bachelor of Arts in English into a job as the supervising cataloguer at their new university's library, now decided to pursue a Master's degree in acting. Having dabbled in some productions during his undergraduate years and frankly bored and frustrated with his job, he dove into acting because he was so thrilled and inspired by Shirley Church, intellectually and artistically, in ways he had never been before in his life.

As part of his acceptance into the program, it was agreed that Malcolm could not be a student in any of Eddie's dramatic literature, history, critical analysis, or playwriting classes. Instead, he would either take those courses when taught by the department's other professors or as an independent study under their supervision. Eddie was, in fact, the one who had proposed that condition. Because of it, Malcolm was given more occasions to have Shirley as his instructor.

He thrived under her tutelage. It was apparent to everyone, especially to Eddie and her, that he had innate gifts as an actor. She cast him as the cynical, alcoholic wastrel son Jamie Tyrone in the spring semester's production of *Long Day's Journey Into Night*. There were murmurs and jokes from some of the theater and general faculty ("There must have been a Black janitor at that convent!" "Well, now we know why he drinks so much!"). And a few students were honestly confused as to how a white father and mother could conceive one son who was White and another Black. But most everyone else accepted the casting without comment. Many were enthusiastic in the realization of what it portended on so many levels not only for the Theater Department, but for the university itself.

Malcolm's attractiveness and magnetism, combined with his intuitive empathy, made him compelling to watch on stage. He traversed Jamie's carousing high spirits and false bravado, his caustic self-pity and alcoholic self-hate, his brotherly tenderness and emotional bullying. Malcolm revealed the man still yearning resentfully and longingly for his father's approval. His skin color lost its primacy to most of the audience; it was there, but not there.

From then on, almost every production cast actors of different races and ethnicities. Enrollment by students of color in acting classes kept rising, and three more declared theater as their major.

In her fourth year, Professor Shirley Church took her most audacious gamble. Despite some vocalized doubt and, in a few cases, outright wishes for failure, she bookended the start of the fall and the end of the spring semesters with two separate productions of *Othello* and a risky, racially charged concept.

She announced in the fall how both were to be cast. The first production would be traditionally presented with Malcolm, who was already beginning to show signs of his illness, starring as the Moor. He would be the only Black actor surrounded by an all-white ensemble. She had strongly considered the idea of casting Professor Edward Duncan as Othello in blackface, wanting to bring *that* tradition to the forefront of her conception but thought the better of it, never letting him know her idea. Although she was certain Eddie would have happily seized the role, she knew she could not risk alienating and losing the Black community on—and off—campus if the two productions were to work in all the ways she wanted.

For the autumn one, Shirley enjoined other professors and instructors in the Theater, English, Humanities, Psychology, and Sociology departments in how to conduct class discussions of the play, especially regarding race, focusing on how each of the white characters treated Othello based on their individual assumptions and projections about his Blackness. In addition, she provided the teachers with her own written class plans on how to guide students' attention on the false face of white Iago, to examine the motives and means of his betrayal of the friendship given to him by the naive, guileless Othello. And, whenever possible, to draw them into considering whether this betrayal (or a fear of betrayal) was something they had experienced or felt possible in their own relationships with friends and classmates, especially those of other races.

Malcolm gave a thunderous performance. He never lost the center of Othello's tragic poignancy—a man, at heart, too innocent and trusting of the white culture that had raised him up as warrior commander, even as he was consumed by his own jealousy and wounded rage. "It confirmed for me that I was an actor who could have succeeded professionally," he said with contented matter-of-factness a couple of weeks before his death. "I proved to myself I was an artist."

Before this fall semester production had even held auditions, Professor Church let it also be known that the second production in spring would feature a *white* Othello as the only Caucasian in the cast. Black theater students would be given the opportunity to delve into the poetry and passions of such rich characters as Iago, Desdemona, Cassio, Roderigo, and Emilia—Shakespearean roles they had never before imagined as possibilities for themselves to play. And pretty much any Black student who auditioned was ensured a role. This would encourage those nonmajors who would never have taken the risk to do so.

But her most brilliant strategic move was opening auditions to Black actors outside of the university. In her first year in Iowa, Shirley had been invited as the guest speaker at the one African American social and cultural organization of the small town that revolved around the university. The audience was charmed by her natural warmth and humor, her lack of pretension—so different from the white professors from the university they had invited to speak before. She didn't condescend, as if they needed help to understand her. The fascinating research and knowledge she provided about their people's history in the theatrical arts electrified them. Shirley was soon invited to become a member of the organization's board. Having placed roots in the university and the community around it, she knew or was known by every prominent person of color.

Shirley enlisted all of them to put the word out that Black actors were needed for crowd scenes and minor speaking roles. Those outside the university also could audition for the major roles in case there weren't enough capable actors on campus to fill them. This was an unprecedented chance to be on the "big stage" of the university theatre.

Of course, Shirley knew this meant a new audience, not normally interested in the department's plays, would be created by the attendance of families, friends, coworkers, and even fellow parishioners of the non-university Black cast. It was an incredibly proud event for all the students and the town's Black community to not only be on stage in major roles in a Shakespeare play, but in one directed by a respected Black professor. Tickets sold out so fast that the department added an extra weekend of performances.

The race reversal of roles turned out to be something far more than the "attention-getting, self-serving stunt" it had been minimized as by some of the more dogmatic and bigoted members of the academic ranks. Rather, it provided an intriguing, provocative prism to examine the seething destructiveness of white paranoia even more than the earlier production of autumn.

Professor Edward Duncan, for one, had never heard so many students of all races so excited and involved about one of the university's productions. "I had the first sustained classroom discussion of a Shakespeare play with nontheater majors in my life. The entire fifty minutes!" one adjunct remarked with dumbfounded delight. He was proud of Professor Shirley Church. She turned the cliche into dynamic reality—Shakespeare was still relevant, could still speak directly to a contemporary, diverse audience.

Shirley wrote a lengthy article about the two productions for a prestigious scholarly journal that was later expanded into a book. While no best-seller, it still sold far more copies than usual for such an academic tome while also receiving excellent reviews. However, she did not write about the dropped idea of casting Professor Edward Duncan in blackface for the production nor did she mention that she almost cast him for the role in the second one as a white Othello surrounded by Blacks.

The increased enrollment, the new audience, the creativity, the policy innovations, the well-regarded and popular book made Shirley Church a star in the insular world of academia. She won tenure easily and received a substantial salary bump commensurate with her standing, and competitive with the offers used to woo her by other universities. She had no ambition to be the department head anywhere. She just wanted to keep on working with the students, especially those of color, and trying out as many ideas on stage with as wide a range of works as possible.

The only scar of the entire event was Malcolm's inability to take on the role of Iago in the second production as she had planned. Unable to muster all the energy and commitment the part necessitated, he withdrew. He was dead the next year.

♦♦♦

Professor Shirley Church snapped Professor Edward Duncan out of the past and propelled him back into the present. "You stopped being on the right side, Eddie."

He roused himself. "You mean stopped being on your side."

"You haven't been on my side for a long time."

"You don't need me on your side. At least, not anymore. You win them all. That's the problem. Every time you win there's one next thing. One more needed proposal. One more needed change. Another item on the agenda."

He then noticed a slight brown stain on the cuff of his sky-blue shirt. Most likely coffee. He wondered how long it had been there, ignored.

Shirley felt a jolt of ire. He still held churlish resentments about her most recent transformations within the Theater Department. "Just because we made color-blind casting acceptable didn't mean we had ensured it as the norm. Requiring every production to cast at least one minority actor in a prominent role was the only way to do so. And truthfully, Eddie, has it been that difficult to find worthy, talented nonwhite winners and finalists since we enacted the new rules on the department's contests and honors awards?"

"That's not my point at all," he said with a patronizing tone that was entirely intentional this time.

"Because in the six years since it was formalized, we have found at least one, and often more than one, nonwhite winner, runner-up, or honorable mention almost every time, even in the blind submissions for the playwriting and design contests." She talked at ferocious speed, ready to make a persuasive case once more for the already enacted policy.

"It's those contests when it's not 'almost every time' that disgusts me, and you know it," Eddie spit out. "Rare as they may be, those times when we have to go back and back and back to find at least one minority student as an honorable mention, it's unfair to every other legitimate white student entry that would have that place," he said equally insistent, equally ready to battle it all over again.

"For how many decades since this university was founded were nonwhite, or 'minority' students as you keep calling them, especially Black students, denied opportunity—any opportunity, *all* opportunity—to compete, much less to win or place, for prizes that were *always* eligible for, *always* awarded to, white students? It's right, and it's just to ensure that institutional racism like that is never allowed to flourish again."

"Christ Jesus, Shirley. You sound like a parody."

His meanness was stinging, but even more, it was enraging—that arrogant dismissiveness, that assumed superiority that he knew more, he knew better. That *whiteness.* "Malcolm would not like what you've become," she said coldly.

"What my dead lover would like or not like is none of your goddamned business, Professor Church. Don't use him to justify you."

"Why not? You certainly do when it suits you, Professor Duncan."

He could not hide the involuntary flinch that crossed his face. She had successfully struck, but there was no happiness in her victory; she could not bear that this was the way they now went at each other most days. They stared frankly at one another, both implacable, both refusing to step back from the precipice over which they now seemed destined to fall.

*Or had they already fallen?* Eddie pondered. He had stood up from his chair without realizing it, so sat down again, propping a yellow cushion behind his back. Looking down, he discovered a second stain, this one on the shirt's midsection overhanging his protruding belly. Red. Ketchup? Why had he not seen this before? He closed his eyes and sighed.

Shirley found her way back to the chair opposite his desk. They both studied the silver-framed picture of still-beaming, forever joyous Malcolm for what seemed a long silent time.

Finally, Eddie spoke, calm and exact. "This new proposal about student written productions takes it all one step too far, Shirley. You're forcing the students to write plays with characters they don't want. You're taking away their choices as artists in order to get their work on stage. It's wrong. Morally and aesthetically and, yes, even politically and socially, wrong. I would almost call it evil."

"Now who's being a parody?" But Shirley tried to rally a softer chiding, some old fondness, in the tenor of her response.

"For all my falling into parody as the bitter curmudgeon and failed professor who has no illusions that he'll ever discover a great new American playwright of this or any other generation, I do take my job seriously, Shirley. As bad, derivative, and pretentious and overwritten and underwritten as the student plays may be, they are an attempt at something. That struggle for their own voice to come out. To be heard as their own. I can't allow that to be taken away from them."

She knew he was sincere. He believed in what he said. It was without rancor and, perhaps ultimately, without racism. But she knew in her bones that it was also limited. *He cannot see how oblivious he is to something larger than his idealized conception of what art is, what art means, what art can do,* she thought to herself. Her longing to make him see, make him understand, was gentler now.

Shirley spoke carefully, almost soothingly. "All that's being asked is that the students who want to produce their scripts on any of our stages must include at least one nonwhite or one non-heterosexual character. Or one character of nonnormative abilities. The playwriting students can write all they want about cis-gendered heterosexual-identified normative-abled white males to their hearts' content. Just as long as they also write a character different than that—Asian, Latinx, transgender, autistic, or any other kind of human being. That's not so much to demand, is it?" She decided to tease him lightly, hoping to coax a smile. "Perhaps someone will even be inspired to write an old white gay male curmudgeon. The new policy simply forces more of the playwriting students to engage in the lives of people unlike themselves."

"That 'forces' is the key word, though, isn't it?" he queried, irritable and on edge. "You're not talking about a classroom assignment. You're talking about refusing production of the white playwriting students' plays..."

"No!" she interrupted. "Refusing to produce *any* playwriting students' play..."

"...unless they have included at least one prominent minority character which is..."

"...that doesn't reflect the makeup of the world as it is..."

"...which is dictating to artists—even young, stupid, or barely talented ones—what they can and cannot create."

She felt as if she would leap across the desk and slap the obtuse, obstinate old white man with the full weight of her fury. But Professor Shirley Church drew on her battered, though still vast, resources of determined purpose to keep herself on track.

"They can write whatever they want. But as part of a university and a community, they must reflect the university and the community if they want their work to be performed on our stages. We're demanding the students to broaden their world."

"You mean the white students. The same white students I've heard you routinely criticize as being too privileged and sheltered to know or comprehend Black lives."

"And this is a way to push them to discover and know those lives. And the lives of others unlike themselves."

Professor Edward Duncan knew it was a lost cause. He would never moderate, much less alter, her stern, unyielding belief in how art must serve change, at least the art of their Theater Department's playwriting students. But he persisted because she wanted to turn this belief into stated, written, enforceable policy. "You're dictating what they can write. It's the ultimate violation."

"No!" she pounced. "Slavery. Rape. Forever living in the legacy of that history, that institutionalized history...that's the ultimate violation. Like most great white liberals, Eddie, you refuse to see how layered and entrenched, how...how...*permanent* it all is. And always will be unless we confront every variation and pulse of it that shows up and blast away the conditions that keep it entrenched."

"And according to you I am the living, breathing embodiment of that entrenchment. 'The last old white male desperately fighting to hold back the inevitable future of our campus.' I think that's your tweet verbatim."

"That wasn't my tweet."

"But it was what you said. To a *student* for God's sake! Who then spread it out on that precocious entity known as Twitter," he fired back.

"I was explaining to him why the playwrights' production policy still hasn't been approved. How you're the one who keeps stalling it. I certainly didn't encourage him to tweet out what I said to him. I had no idea he would do that," she insisted with a hint of defensiveness. "But let's face it, Eddie. You *are* the last old white male holding back the inevitable future."

He fixed on her with a barely detectable sneer. "You're right, of course. That's my role now. The white dinosaur who 'just doesn't get it.' Over forty years of pushing for you, for other minorities, for gays and lesbians, or I guess I should now say 'queers.' Pushing for so many changes. Pushing for the importance of theater and all the arts in this football-soaked mediocrity called a university. Forty years of student plays read and guided. All the productions directed, trying to make some type of meaning, and, yes, some kind of art, minor but real, with the students who cared, who sincerely desired to learn, to be better. At the very least, make some little stage 'magic' and entertainment, as quaint as those notions are to you who believe social engineering is the only noble purpose of the arts. The decades and decades I've put in with all the students and the backstabbing academic politics and the loss of Malcolm. All of it. *Reduced.* Here I am, a 'meme' for this week's outraged social media 'hot takes,' for the internet's self-appointed, self-justifying 'cultural critics' to dissect and caricature and condemn. The last old white male holding back the inevitable future. That's my legacy for all of it according to you."

"And now you hope to turn the table and make me the outrage," Shirley replied sharply, brandishing the list of the faculty meeting agenda.

A mild half-smile flickered across his lips. "You did that one to yourself. I'm just taking advantage of the opening you gave me."

"And lucky you, you didn't even have to sully yourself by going on social media to exploit it."

"I have sunk exceptionally low and done some awful things in my lifetime, Professor Church. Still, I haven't yet sunk low enough to be part of all that nonsense. The one promise I've made to myself is to die without ever having a Facebook page, Twitter account, or a set of selfies on Instagram. That's the world you play in."

Shirley felt the surging rush once again to slap him hard and terrible across his white face. "You're not going to get the faculty to censure me over some inane controversy about the Academy Awards, Eddie," she scoffed.

"You, of all people, are not that naive. It may have been about the Academy Awards, a mere contrarian opinion which, for whatever it's worth, used to be one of my favorite things about you. But you know damn well that's not how it's playing out on Twitter. I do read the internet on occasion," he said, jerking his head toward the computer.

He spotted yet another stain. Something dark and crusty on the upper thigh of his wrinkled khaki Dockers, a pair of pants he had owned for some twenty years. Perhaps it was chocolate. Or mud? Why had none of these caught his attention until now?

"It was a silly, stupid tweet." Shirley waved her elongated hands, shooing his words away.

But Eddie perceived nicks in her confidence. "The university is now under fire for having you on faculty. There are even calls for you to resign."

"No one is going to fire me over an opinion that was, at worst, flippant."

"No, Shirley. It was more than flippant. It was 'trivializing' and 'contemptuous.' Against another African American woman." He pulled a yellow legal pad filled with his handwriting from atop one of the piles on his desk. "I quote, 'So get hashtag OscarsSoWhite. But I may be the only Black woman who's not impressed by Ava DuVernay or upset that she didn't nab an undeserved Best Director nomination for *Selma*.' You made a racist, misogynist attack on her according to the arbiters of Twitter, feminist Twitter, Black Twitter, and Black feminist Twitter," Eddie snorted.

"Of all people, I have the most right, maybe the *only* right, to tweet an opinion like that." Shirley heard the scolded little girl pleading in her voice and despised herself for it.

Eddie was sickened by his own pettiness in pressing on in this direction, but he could not help himself. It felt cathartic to be able to push back against her using this particular weapon. "Well, it seems like many others, especially respected, published Black feminist academic women, vehemently disagree with you."

"I just didn't like the movie," she protested. "And you don't give a shit about any of it. It's just something to use against me, hoping it will stop the policy change with the playwriting students."

Eddie's hard-headed, hard-hearted bluster deflated. He did not want to go on like this any longer. He could hear his unkindness. His cheap, small spitefulness. Shirley had been under attack for a week by what seemed like the entire world, or at least that entire ether world known as social media. He was kicking her more, adding to it. Shirley, with whom he had shared work and laughter and right and valid achievements for some thirty-five years. Shirley, who had been so good to Malcolm, especially as he was dying, and so good to Eddie himself afterward, comforting him as he sobbed in her arms.

When he finally spoke, he hoped to at least be clear as to his true divide with her so she would see there was no racial, and certainly no personal, animosity in his stance. His tone was muted but affectionate. "Shirley is my big-hearted, funny, brilliant, and formidable friend. Shirley is the reason I've been able to go on for so long after Malcolm with this theater department and the students. Shirley is someone I still treasure very much. But...well...Professor Church. She's someone I disagree with on nearly everything she says and does these days. And her imposing an agenda that has nothing to do with art, that is the very antithesis of art, is repugnant to everything I believe about art and its creation. The torches and pitchfork uproar from the social media mob demanding censure for her 'problematic' tweet is a bad, ugly joke that no one should be paying any attention to. Shirley doesn't deserve that. Still, if it can bring to a halt, or even just further delay, Professor Church's didactic policy dictating what the students must write so they can be produced on our campus stages...if it can be used as a bargaining chip...then yes, I embrace these ends justifying those means. But please. Please know that my quarrel is not with Shirley, but only with Professor Church."

Shirley's stiffening back and hardened gaze generated a great unease within him. He averted his face. And then found more stains splotched on his clothes, blots of all sizes and all colors. He now knew his dream of restoring a connection with Shirley while divorcing Professor Church in some amicable, understanding fashion was not to be realized.

Shirley rose from the chair in a single shiver of energy. Her voice was charged and tense, but she enunciated her words with unwavering precise steeliness. "You're patronizing me and you're lying to yourself. You want me to believe this is all some principled disagreement. But the item on today's agenda is about punishment. And not just punishment for disagreeing with you. I know that now."

"What on earth could this be about but our differences?"

"I've been doing substantive, transformative work on the racial policies and practices of this department and of this university for decades. And I'm charging forward and going further with what still needs to be done to address the institutional racism so intrinsic to all of it. More than hating my doing it, you hate the fact that I'm *successful* doing it. Successful doing it *without you*."

"You think this is all about nothing but professional jealousy?"

"Oh, I don't think it's jealousy, Eddie," she said, her eyes boring into him mercilessly. "You hate that I don't need you anymore. You hate that I don't need your voice backing up mine to legitimize my work to make change happen. You being the white savior. You hate losing your role."

"You're being simplistic and reductive. As always," he replied with a hostility he had never let anyone hear before. "Stop wrapping yourself up in that fur coat of self-complimenting aggrandizement, Shirley."

But she was feeling the pleasure of release, of at last saying what she had known for many years but had not dared to ever speak. She could live with the truth and whatever its consequences, and to hell with Professor Eddie Duncan if he could not.

"You hate I'm not that idealistic, awkward, trying-so-hard-to-please young Black girl just out of graduate school who didn't know how to negotiate this white academic world to get what she wanted, what her students *needed*, from it. I won't apologize for that, Eddie."

"It's been a very long time since I've heard you apologize for anything," he spat out.

"You don't want me to apologize for some dumb tweet about Ava DuVernay's Oscar chances. You want me to apologize for surpassing you. It's not just that I make change without you. You hate that I'm doing it *beyond* you. Beyond your abilities and understanding. Perhaps even beyond Malcolm's."

Eddie knew they had fallen off the precipice. They would hit the hard, unforgiving earth and be broken. "So even Malcolm would fail to grasp your deeply moral and intellectual deconstruction of our 'ingrained institutionalized racism.' Even *he* would not be able to appreciate the logic and rightness of your rigid racial corrections."

Shirley realized that they had fallen off the precipice too. So, there was no need to stop now. "Malcolm was Black. And he was gay. And he was HIV-positive. But he was a *man*," she asserted, emphasizing a cutting disdain for the very concept. "With a white lover. So, yes. Even he might not have fully understood these issues. Could not grasp how art refuses to intimately and inextricably link racism and homophobia."

Eddie jumped up and roared with indignation. "Malcolm and I didn't need art to understand that intimate and inextricable link of racism and homophobia. We learned all we needed to every time he was called a 'snowball-chasing faggot' by Black people, and I was called a 'nigger-lover' by white ones!"

Shirley gasped. She stepped back as if physically punched. They stood, both quiet and breathing hard, both reeling. He wanted to go to her, to embrace and comfort her in her humiliation and hurt. But her self-possessed composure swiftly returned. She stood ramrod straight and lifted her head regally. Livid as she was, she was not about to allow him to see her own unbridled emotions.

"After all these years as your friend. After all these years as your colleague and peer. To say that word to me."

Shaken by his own outburst, Eddie was nevertheless certain he had done no wrong. "I didn't call you that word. I said it to describe what I've been called. That's the context."

"Your context. Not mine," she heatedly shot back.

"I just said I've had a phrase with the n-word in it hurled at me. That's the truth of my experience."

"That doesn't give you any allowance to say that word to me. *Ever.* To make that word part of *my* experience today or any day."

"All I said to you was fact."

"You're going to drop this. Now," Shirley proclaimed, holding up the meeting's agenda.

Eddie knew what she was doing and wanted to pretend he did not. Still, he inquired, "Are you going to drop your policy proposal regarding the playwriting students and their productions?"

"No. Never," she replied, more adamant and immovable than ever.

"Then I'm not dropping the item about your censure."

She moved closer to him, leaning into his face, her eyes ablaze. "Then I'm adding another item for today. A motion for your immediate resignation for using the n-word." She was almost whispering.

"I did not call you the n-word," he bellowed.

Shirley's voice reverberated with contempt. "In ways you don't know and will never understand, Eddie, Professor Edward Duncan, yes, yes you did." She turned, ready at last to leave the claustrophobic, airless office. In fact, she was suddenly seized with a crazy panic that she might never get out of it.

"You might be able to impress your gullible students and some star-struck young lesbians on the faculty with that kind of semantic shell game, Professor Church, but the fact, the truth, is I did not call you the n-word." Hate coursed through him.

Swinging around to face him once more, Shirley's hate was equal to his. "We can let the rest of the world come to its own conclusions about that when my motion becomes public. Disseminated through Twitter, of course." As his white skin turned even paler, she felt the triumph. "To be known as the white male professor who says the n-word to a Black female professor is a lot more controversy and uproar for the university to deal with than a Black woman saying another Black woman doesn't deserve an Oscar nomination. What I've put up with in the last week is nothing compared to what will be done to you." She brandished the knife she knew would cut deepest. "You could even lose your retirement."

Eddie was stunned. But more than that, for the first time, he was genuinely terrified. "You would really do this to me? Without my retirement, I have nothing." He again became aware that he had stood up at some point without realizing he had done so. He dropped into his chair, disoriented, drowning.

Shirley felt a tremor of shame for how scared he now seemed. In the 1990s, when Malcolm died of AIDS, Eddie's finances had been decimated. Of course, he had no claim to Malcolm's Social Security as a widower back then. Some compassion resurfaced within her. She slowly came up to his chair and knelt beside him. She tentatively placed her hand upon his arm. She paused, doubting, but then let her instincts override all else. "You could announce your retirement for the end of the semester at today's meeting," she urged helpfully. "If you add that item to today's agenda, I'll have no need to add mine."

He looked down at her huge hands on his arm. "You trying to be friends now?" Eddie grunted, swiftly and harshly pulling his arm away.

Taken aback, Shirley froze. But only momentarily. She raised herself from the crouching position, her poised assurance returned. "I'll drop my proposal for the playwrights' productions change. At least for now. I promise. I won't pursue it until next semester. After you're gone."

Slowly, Professor Edward Duncan turned his bleary blue-gray eyes to meet her own dark brown ones, which now seemed all-black pupils to him. His voice was strong and decisive, without any other emotion. "I will not be blackmailed out of my old white male principles. Get the fuck out of my office, Professor Church."

She refused to be dissuaded. "You've got the rest of the afternoon to decide, Professor Duncan. Drop the censure motion. Announce your resignation for the end of the semester. Otherwise, I have no other choice but to press for your being fired for saying the n-word to me."

He picked up a student paper and pretended to read. He rummaged through his mind and found the word he knew would be the cruelest. "You're *dismissed*, Professor Church."

Shirley realized she pitied him more than she hated him. He had once been someone important, even special, to her life. But since this was their end, she would say the unsayable of many decades.

"You loved Malcolm very much, Eddie. I know that. But I don't think you knew him at all. I was sorry for him. You didn't ever really know him and never could. Even at the time he was dying."

Professor Shirley Church opened the door and walked out of the office, closing it behind her exactly as the silver-framed photo of the sublimely smiling and life-embracing Malcolm was hurled against it, glass shattering into so many shards and pieces. It had been thrown with all the force and ferocity, all the sorrow and grief, of a lifetime's war. A war, both within and without, over sexuality, race, love, loss, yes. But more about the broken, craving human heart than could ever be articulated, much less salved, by the comfort of art or the effort of creating it.

# American Horror Story

Ally is having her revenge on Ivy, the wife who tried to drive her insane with a nightmarish cult of killer clowns.

It's *American Horror Story*, the one television show you never miss. The only series you must watch in real-time, no matter what else is going on that evening. You even turn your phone off for it.

Ivy is retching up thick black bloody bile. Ally has poisoned her, putting arsenic in the pasta sauce. Ivy falls, shocked and wild-eyed in the realization of what is happening.

"There are only two things I want in my life," Ally says, cool and impassive. "To have full custody of my son and to watch you die."

Ivy writhes on the floor in death throes, spewing more thick black bloody bile. There's a bemused, satisfied twinkle in Ally's eyes as she holds up her glass of white wine in a modest toast to her pleasure. "Halfway there," she says.

You burst out laughing, horrified and appalled. It's exactly what you most love about the show! Yes, it's camp twisted fun, but it also makes you shudder with a terror that entertains you.

Besides, Ivy got everything she deserved.

◆◆◆

The following morning there are police and medical personnel outside your sixth-floor apartment going up and down the hallway. Bright school-bus yellow tape emblazoned in bold black capital letters repeatedly proclaiming **CRIME SCENE DO NOT CROSS** stretches from wall-to-wall, blocking anyone else from passage further down.

Kevin, the man in the apartment down the hall at the furthest end of the floor, has been found dead, slashed and stabbed multiple times with a jagged stainless-steel kitchen knife, his blood splattered and smeared everywhere—the floor, the walls, the furniture.

He was kind. A handsome man in his early forties, he looked a good ten years younger. Genuinely friendly, always stopping to chat for a few minutes as you crossed paths in the elevator or at the mailboxes in the downstairs lobby.

Even though you really didn't know him all that well.

You find out in his obituary later that he had worked hard ever since he was a teenager in a small, poor town in Missouri, joining the Marines right out of high school and serving for eight years. He then put himself through college and graduate school, becoming a highly successful software designer at a major tech company in the Bay Area. He loved going to Burning Man, would bike hundreds of miles through the Montana mountains, and played shortstop for a team in the San Francisco Gay Softball League.

He was murdered by his boyfriend. A twenty-something dancer in a modest but well-regarded local troupe. Dark-skinned. *Was he Brazilian? Italian? Egyptian?* The boyfriend, whose name you could never remember—something complex and difficult to pronounce—was far more excitable and emotional, extravagant even, in his speech and manner than the more plain-spoken, easygoing Kevin.

It was impossible not to notice their differences.

Kevin's death is confirmed by the boyfriend as occurring the previous evening. Right around the time you were riotously laughing over Ally's triumphant murder of Ivy.

♦♦♦

You skip next week's episode of *American Horror Story*.

Maybe you'll stream it later, watching on a smaller screen.

# This is Enough

Yesterday I looked at myself naked in the mirror. Really looked from the top of my head all the way down to my toes. It felt super gross knowing that almost every inch of my body has been...*traveled* by somebody else. I hate that.

When I looked myself in the face, tried to see all the way inside my eyes, I knew that the baseball-playing, skateboarding, bad-at-math little kid Johnny, *their* Johnny—my Mom and Dad's Johnny—*that* Johnny was gone and was never ever going to come back again. If I showed up now after everything that's happened and all the years passed, I'd be taking their Johnny away from them all over again. That's not fair.

The part that I don't think anybody would understand is that it wasn't all bad. Or not always bad. That's the better way to put it. I mean, weeks, months would go by, and I was in so much pain and so damned lonely and sad all the time that I just wanted to die. To be totally out of it. But...it's hard to explain. There would be other times, other things.

Like when nobody bothered me for weeks at a time. No sex, no weirdness. I was basically left alone. I got to just hang out. Play all the best games I wanted on a ginormous TV. Sleep as much as I wanted and read comic books all day. Even play around outside. Go swimming in a pool and finally getting to wear trunks.

There were times like the first time I got to see the ocean. In Hawaii! Gigantic and so fucking blue, a blue I had never seen before and haven't seen anywhere else since. I know it sounds strange, but it was like a magical blue. I don't know how else to say it. But staring and staring at the ocean, I felt like I became that blue. That was great.

And there were other times. Getting to camp out. Fishing. Nothing expected, nothing happening. No sex stuff or creepy stuff. Friendly guys who did kind of remind me of Dad.

There was one time even when this old guy, like grandpa old, gave me a back rub all over my body, but he didn't grab like all the others. His hands were so strong and big, warm even. But not rough, and not pinching and sneaking like other times with guys. Just nice strong hands using some sort of lotion that smelled so good. And he took his time rubbing my neck and shoulders and back and legs and feet. It felt so good having my feet rubbed. It wasn't all sexed up. He never touched my dick or did anything to my butt. It was almost like he was helping me have my body again. I wasn't invisible to him.

It's not like I'm saying, "Well, at least there were some…*benefits* about it all that made it OK." Those few good things don't even out all the horrible things. The sick stuff. They don't! That's not possible. It's just that good things still happened, and I couldn't help but like it when they did. There were so many terrible, nasty, pervert things that went on. So, I decided to just enjoy and really appreciate anything that was genuinely good, that felt good.

There was one time when I might have been able to escape. But I didn't take the chance. I'm not sure people would understand that either. Partly because I was so afraid. Getting my dick and balls cut off was the threat they made the most, and there were times when I was tied up, and they played with big knives like they were going to do it. I think some of them would have if some of the others hadn't stopped them.

We were in the parking lot of a mall not far from the highway. Our car was near the doors of the big main entrance. They told me not to make a sound or get noticed. But it would have been so easy. Even with the dark windows all rolled up and the doors locked. Because they went in and left me alone. Maybe because they were afraid of how I might act in public or maybe because I looked too weird by that point.

Anyway, my wrists and ankles were handcuffed to a chain bolted to the floor, and my mouth was taped. I could see people were walking all over the parking lot, going in and out of the big doors. If I had just rammed my head as hard and as strong as I could against the window, I might have been able to smash it. Just ram it through the glass and break it open. At least I could make enough noise trying, so somebody would hear and maybe help me find a way to get out.

I swear I thought of doing that. But I just couldn't. I wasn't brave enough. I was so near freedom after all that time and all that had happened to my body. But I froze.

None of this makes any sense, I know. But I had gotten to a point where I couldn't see myself anymore without them. Somehow, as much as it was all so crazy and awful, I knew it had also become my life. It was what I knew most by then and I was starting to get confused when I tried picturing my first life. I wasn't sure how I could go back to it. Probably because I knew most everybody—Mom, Dad, my gang from school...shit, total strangers even—they all would end up knowing what kind of things had happened. What kind of things had been done to me. What kind of things I had done. Everybody would look at me and point and know too much about me. About my body. I didn't want all those eyes, all that attention, put on me.

The craziest moment, the time where I think I may have lost my mind for a little while, was one of the times I did the dog thing. The dog thing was the thing I always hated the most. I had to be naked, of course. They had me on my hands and knees and kept yanking me with this thick, black, spiked collar around my neck. I had to bark every time they yanked, and every time I barked, they slashed my butt hard with this thin leather thing that cut like fire. But I couldn't cry or say anything. I could howl or whimper. But no yelling, no words. No tears. I always had to be the dog.

But this one time when I was doing the dog thing, something happened to me. Once I started barking, I barked gigantic crazy loud. Just barking and barking and barking like a deranged, foaming, rabid mad dog for what seemed like hours. The more I barked, the more they hit me with that cutting leather thing. First on my butt and then all over my back and legs. But for some reason I just couldn't stop when I was supposed to. When I was supposed to come to heel, and then they could fuck me. But I wouldn't...couldn't...stop barking. I wouldn't come to heel. I just kept barking and barking louder and louder, wilder and wilder.

And you know what? The more I barked, the more I felt what it was to be a real dog in a collar on a leash and somebody whips you and whips you and you can't escape. It really could make you go insane to where there would be nothing to do but just bark and bark and bark forever. There was so much I wanted to say that couldn't be kept in any longer that I didn't have any words for. Even if I did, words would never ever be able to say what that barking—that endless, crazy, never-stopping mad-dog barking—said for me. The truth is that barking became like praying.

Almost all of the time, it was men, but a couple of times it was with women. People don't think women do the weird shit or the psycho mean stuff, but man...let me tell you. They *do*! Don't think it wasn't as bad or not as violent just because it was with women.

The sheer happiness some people have in being mean is what fucks my head up the most. How did they get this way? What happened to them to make them become like this? They were once little kids. They didn't just wake up one day and say, "I'm going to start kidnapping and torturing boys," and then go out and do it. They had to have come to some *idea* about it. That this was something they wanted to do. And then they had to plan it. Think of everything down to the last littlest detail very carefully and clearly. And all the time they were coming to their decisions and making all these plans, they must have known it was wrong. Like burn-in-hell wrong. But they just went ahead and did it anyway.

Some of them really do become like animals. They tear through us so wild. Devour. I learned that word once, and it fits so perfectly. "Devour." That's what they do.

I can't believe anybody ever did this kind of thing to them when they were kids because there is no way you would do it to somebody else if you know what it feels like. It's just so goddamn fucking impossible to wrap my head around. They just couldn't have started off their lives this evil.

And sometimes, what's truly scary, is that some of them do things, say things, that kind of prove they aren't. At least not totally.

One time when I was chained naked to a bed, this guy came in. It had been a long ugly party—probably the nastiest and meanest party they ever had—and I was just so damned tired and hurting. I figured he was coming in for more, and I tried to make myself ready, like in my mind, for whatever he was going to do. But, instead, he just looked at me for a long time, longer than anyone of them had ever looked at me, and his eyes just got real open and sad. Like he was the beat dog. I even started to feel kind of sorry for him, which I know is pretty fucked up when you think about it. But I couldn't help myself. I've never seen any person look that sad ever. He was around my Dad's age.

And then he snapped out of it. He got like super busy. First, he undid the cuffs and very, very gently rubbed my wrists. Then he took off his t-shirt. I just lay there thinking he was going to do something. But he gave the t-shirt to me and pulled out some gym shorts from a chest of drawers and told me to put them on even though they were too big for me. And then he left the room for a while but came back with some food—hot tomato soup and a grilled cheese sandwich and a big glass of cold milk—and he told me to eat it slowly, so I wouldn't get sick and throw up. He told me not to worry. That nobody would be bothering me for a long, long time.

Later, he took me to a super-sized bathroom upstairs and said I could take a hot bath or shower for as long as I wanted and that I could even lock the door from the inside. He got so serious and talked very slow, like maybe I was retarded or something. But I think he just wanted to be sure I totally understood and believed him. He promised that there were no hidden cameras or peepholes or one-way mirrors or windows or anything or anyplace where anybody could see me. And then he gave me these wonderful big thick, clean white towels. And brand-new underwear and fresh pajamas. Which kind of made me want to laugh since it had been so long since I had worn pajamas or underwear.

He really wanted to be nice to me. It felt so different from other times when they were nice to me just because they wanted me to act a certain way without having to beat or whip me first. This guy really was trying to think about what I wanted and what I would like.

Later when I went to bed in the master bedroom and the lights were off, he came in. My stomach turned over sick. I was so disappointed and sad. Because I thought, "Uh-oh, here it comes."

But instead, this guy...he just knelt beside the bed and said super soft, "I want you to know that I'll be outside the door the rest of the night. No one is going to come in. No one. I promise. You can sleep for as long and as late as you want and trust that no one is going to come in and bother you or do anything to you. This night and this bed are all yours and yours alone."

I don't know why but my voice got all shaky and emotional, and I almost busted out crying when I said back to him, "Thank you, mister."

He stopped for a moment. And then he said, almost like he was going to bust out crying himself, "I would kill myself before I would kill you."

And spooky as hell as it was, in one way I felt...safe. I trusted him when he said that. Because he said it like it was a *decision*. Something he was sure of. In his own way, he wanted to be very clear with me that that was the way it was. In his own way, he was being kind to me.

So, he left the room. I heard him lock the door. And I slept for probably fourteen hours, I bet. When I woke up and got out of bed, and after I peed, I just lightly knocked on my side of the door. He was still there. And you know what he did? He asked me very politely, "Can I come in to bring you some breakfast?"

I don't know why they didn't kill me. They usually do when you get too old. I was sixteen by the time that guy let me have a night alone after the rough party, and this had all started when I was twelve. Kind of a mind-fuck to think that I didn't even have any hair down there yet, back when they took me. I'll admit, I had played with myself a few times. But I had never even shot a wad before. And the thought of some guy's dick in my mouth? Puke! It was too sickening to even try and picture. Titties and pussies are what I wanted to look at whenever I got a chance when I was a little kid. But to tell the truth, even that seemed sort of gross. Sex was out there, somewhere else. Not part of me all that much. It hadn't kicked in yet. Which is probably why they wanted me, I guess.

So, what happened to me was pretty unusual for sure. You see, a few months later, after that night alone, I was supposed to rape this new kid, fuck him raw, for this big show. Very exclusive rich guys. I had done these parties before with other kids, sometimes even with girls. But I had never done something to someone new. Someone who had never experienced any of it before. Someone who didn't know what it would feel like, what it would do to them, to their soul I guess, the way it had done to me.

The music was loud. Just off-the-charts insane asylum loud. Blaring, deafening, bone-crunching heavy metal stadium rock. And there was this riot of black and white lights flashing like a billion times a second. There was no space to hear your own heartbeat or your own thoughts. It was all so hyper and intense. Monumental, you know? And I was just getting more and more pumped up, excited, madder and madder with all this anger. Fury, to be honest. Like ready to murder. I could feel myself spinning more and more out of control. I was going to give them a show and fuck this kid way past anything that had ever been done to me. And I was going to do it with so much happy, satisfied *rage*.

But when I saw that new kid's eyes for just one split-second...and then another split-second...and then another...in between all those flashing lights, something shuddered inside me. The closer I got to his face so I could see him and really look into his eyes, I saw how watery and blue they were. An incredible blue like that Hawaii ocean. Not saying a word. Just looking at me, begging. Pleading. For some...kindness, I guess.

Everything was so furious and hateful and savage—that pounding loud music, the blinking nightmare lights going on and off like a kind of seizure, the men around the stage yelling out, "Fuck him. Fuck him hard. Make him bleed!"

But suddenly, out of nowhere, I got so quiet inside. My mind stopped going so fast, and none of it sounded loud anymore. I felt like I was going far away from it all even though I was still right there in the center of it. A very slow and steady "No" started growing inside me. A continuous, building "No" that felt so cooling and calming, like an ocean breeze. It felt like it was actually humming in me. I just didn't feel anger anymore.

I didn't move at first. I didn't do anything. But then I went up to the kid and put my arms around him. I hugged him as close and tight but also as gently as I could. And I whispered in his ear, "I'm sorry I can't save you from any of this. But I promise. I would kill myself before I would kill you."

At first, they didn't know what was going on. But the longer nothing happened but me holding that kid, I could feel them getting more and more confused and seething and more...*devouring*. I had fucked up their show, and they were infuriated. They started screaming their guts out. Top-of-their-lungs raving. Louder than the music. I held on to that kid, trying with all my might to protect him from all of it for as long as I possibly could.

I don't know all that happened except I was whipped and kicked and burned and beaten and fucked brutal for so long that I lost track of the days. But when one of them came to shove me some food in the cage one day, as hungry and whipped as I was, that "No" was still burning through me all over inside. It sounds stupid, but even though I could barely move or speak, I felt strong.

That "No" must have been on my face because the guy who brought the food looked at me, sneering like I was a pile of dog shit. He just kept staring at me. Like, forever. Then, the next thing I know, I was yanked out of the cage and being smashed around in a way I never had before.

I thought, "OK, soon enough I'll be dead." But I wasn't afraid. I was honestly peaceful about it. I wanted to live, but I wanted to keep that "No" even more.

And the next thing I see is sky. Cold and cloudless black-blue night sky. And stars. More fucking stars than I have ever seen in my entire life. I thought that maybe I had died, and this was my first glimpse of heaven. That might sound like bullshit, but it's totally true. I thought I was in heaven. I felt happy looking up at those bright white and silver stars shimmering in the sky. Everything was so quiet and still. Just for a flash, I thought I saw those ocean-blue eyes of that kid begging for kindness. And then it was sky and stars again.

I could feel myself breathing with that unrelenting "No" beating time with my heart underneath those billions of stars. For all the pain I was in and for all the confusion as to where I was and what had happened, I kept breathing that "No." I knew I was free.

The one thing I've promised to myself after all this is that I will always try to be kind. Especially to anyone who is helpless. Anybody who has it worse. The Johnny of the mirror wasn't ever supposed to have happened, but he's here now, and there's no way getting around that. So, if nothing else, the least he can do is still be kind. I mean, *I* can still be kind.

There's a lot more I could tell you. A whole lot more. A whole lot worse. You may think you want to know about it all, but believe me, you don't. And even if you really do, you know what? You don't need to know all of it. You don't have the *right* to know all of it. Because it's mine. Not yours. This is enough.

# Obituaries

Kurt Woolen has died. And though I have not seen him, spoken to him, written him, nor made any effort or had any inclination to do so in the four decades since I last sat in front of him in our assigned seats during sophomore English class at Oakford Catholic High School, I feel...*satisfied* at this news. There is no second thought or guilty conscience about it either.

A short, squat boy with a bulldog build, a second-stringer on the football team who rarely played, with his coal-black hair cut close to the scalp, he always wore a sneering, arrogant little grin when I knew him as a teenager. He had lived a hard, mean life of drugs and alcohol, prison, mental illness, and borderline poverty. No cause of death is listed in his obituary from the old hometown newspaper, *The Oakford Daily Journal,* I occasionally read online. I really don't need to know what he died of, though. The fact of his death is enough.

There's no doubt in my mind that Kurt Woolen was a psychopath and always had been. Even as a teenager, I wondered if he had some form of brain damage—dropped on his head by a careless parent, or perhaps severely beaten by one in a rage. But it's impossible to have much sympathy for whatever suffering he himself endured as a child and teenager given the daily torments and violent humiliations he inflicted on me and others he picked as easy prey.

My daily nauseous dread of him in my freshman and sophomore years was not exaggerated and self-dramatizing as a therapist I once saw in my late twenties tried to convince me. A year or two after I had graduated high school and was attending a college blessedly far away from my hometown, friends who remained there informed me that Kurt Woolen had killed a man with a knife during a mutually drunken brawl. He was quickly found guilty on some degree of manslaughter. But for reasons I have no knowledge of, he only served four years in the Kentucky State Penitentiary before returning home. I had been intuitive and entirely reasonable in my fear as a high school student that he might murder me.

Besides hitting me with solid striking blows up against my head, slapping me angrily and repeatedly across my face, slamming me up against brick walls, choking me, and spitting on me while contemptuously mocking me as "sissy," "faggot," and "queer," he once punched me in the balls with his full-force fist. I nearly vomited on the spot in the boys' locker room, where both he and I were naked. No, his dick was not some tiny piece, nor was it a huge wonder. It was average; in fact, pretty much the exact same size as mine. I don't know why, but in my teenage closeted homo mind this made the whole experience all the more shaming.

The same therapist also tried to convince me that this act was Woolen's projected gay-panic over his own same-sex desires. But I've always known that was sheer, unadulterated grade-A bullshit. As if I should somehow find *comfort* or be *complimented* that Kurt Woolen was probably way, way deep down within a hidden, guilt-ridden space of himself a cock-loving faggot just like me.

His angry clenched fist slamming into my groin was about nothing more than his gleeful freedom in how much violence he was allowed to get away with. Even as a lowly freshman and sophomore second-stringer, his status still raised him up in the school's hierarchy as "untouchable" by any other student or teacher, save for the occasional mild discipline by one of the coaches. The most reprimand he ever got from any teacher who witnessed his torture upon me or any other hapless, friendless boy was a sharp, barked "Cut that out!" or "Knock it off." He invariably responded with an ugly little chuckle and a short break in his happy cruelty. That is, until the teacher turned their back to the class or buried their face in lecture notes to avoid confronting him again.

Of course, he knew I was a perfect target—a skinny, unpopular, acne-strewn, and more than fey closeted-to-no-one-but-himself fourteen-year-old.

The news of his dying surprises me in the Pandora's box of memories and old feelings it stirs. From rare mentions of him by friends, I knew he lived with his mother in his childhood home after being released from prison and that he was obviously mentally unstable, an alcoholic and a meth addict. But even that information was a couple of decades old by the time I read his obituary. Kurt Woolen had not been entirely forgotten by me, but there had been no real reason to think of him either.

No wife or children, living or dead, are listed in his obituary, although close to a dozen names of siblings predeceasing or surviving him take up the bulk of it. I am struck by the odd omission of one piece of family genealogy, that inescapable component of one's life in a small Southern town: there is no name or identification given of his father at all.

The other thing that stands out for me in this online write-up is that the upcoming funeral Mass will be said by Father Gabriel Dunn. Gabe Dunn was also our classmate. And the first boy I had ever fallen in love, or at least love's closest approximation for a naive, frightened homosexual teenager in early 1970s Kentucky. Gabe was tall and gangly, a popular and surprisingly skilled basketball player. He had thick, curly reddish hair always falling over his puppy-brown eyes, a shy broad smile, and a painfully awkward disposition outside of the ball court, stammering and rarely looking anyone in the eye. I wonder now if he would be considered mildly autistic.

While Gabe might have sensed my great crush on him, nothing was ever acknowledged by either of us. Except for a brief senior-year relationship with Maureen Harris, our high school's free-spirit hippie girl—she wore fringed brown leather vests over virgin white peasant blouses and purple headbands adorned with peace signs—he was never known to be romantically (much less sexually) involved with anyone, girl or boy. Not even a rumor. Still, one of the most fervent erotic memories of my life, seared into my psyche forever, is of spending the night at his home our junior year (separate beds, separate rooms) and finding his discarded white jockey briefs bunched in the corner of the family bathroom. I so wanted to pick up that wadded underwear and bring it into my face, breathing in what I imagined Gabe's musky crotch must smell like. The temptation was a thrilling mixture of hot rising lust and damning Catholic sinfulness that was so exquisite I just couldn't make myself cross the line to know its actual consequence. But for many, many years I ecstatically jerked off to the heated imprint of that resisted fantasy, visualizing Gabe's lanky naked body with its thin curlicue of just-budding pubic hair and slender long cock, glanced in the showers after freshman year gym class. It was the closest I ever got to having sex with him.

Since Gabe lived in the same neighborhood as Kurt Woolen on the poorer east side of Oakford, they attended the same Catholic grade school. Because he was such a good and valuable basketball player, he was not misused or taunted by Woolen and other boys of that ilk in their eight years of shared classrooms. Though he was not one of them—too clumsy off-court and withdrawn and mumbling and prayerful—they left him alone and even cheered and whooped for him as he scored amazing rebounds on the basketball court. Even as a child,

Gabe always carried an obvious sensitivity that was recognized by both the nuns and his fellow students as being genuinely religious.

The last interaction I had with Gabe Dunn was at Oakford Catholic High School's Class of 1972 Twentieth-Year Reunion. Finally confident enough in my physical attractiveness, and even confident enough in my emotional maturity to handle whatever his reaction might be, I decided to subtly engage Father Gabe in intimate conversation. Since I knew I would not see him again for several years, if ever, I thought, "Why not?" I covertly tried to steer our conversation into a revelation of secrets and still-held desires, most pointedly his. I was curious if any awareness of homosexuality had dawned since high school and whether he had acted upon some portion of it. If nothing else, getting my high school crush, now a priest, into bed during a twenty-year class reunion would make a great story to tell my friends in San Francisco, where I now lived.

But somewhere along the fifth or sixth beer I drank during our talk, which had moved to a walnut-paneled side room of the pretentious country club the reunion was being held, I was moved toward some misguided effort of returning to my spiritual "roots." I made a heartfelt request for penance, the very sacrament itself. I spoke guiltily of a young man some ten years my junior who I had treated callously a few years earlier in my first rush of success and big money. To his credit, Father Gabe expressed no reproach or judgment, only asking if there was any way I could contact this young man to tell him directly of my failure in being decent and fair to him. Perhaps I could offer to help him with his education and career or assist with the costs for any counseling or rehabilitation services he might need.

I promised to try and locate this ex-lover and see what I could do to make amends. After a sincere, stumbling effort at praying the Act of Contrition I remembered in peculiar starts and stops, Father Gabe, as the Catholic Church's ordained representative of Jesus Christ on earth, forgave me for my great sin of having a fucked-up relationship in my early thirties.

The next morning, hungover, I felt far more remorse at having participated in that self-abasing sacramental act than I did at any mistreatment I had perpetrated on my former lover. Despite periodic visits to Oakford to spend time with family and long-time friends, I have done nothing to see or speak with Father Gabe nor have I ever run into him again. For that matter, I've never attended another high school reunion either.

Nevertheless, once I returned to San Francisco after that drunken, misbegotten confession, I felt compelled to complete my penance. I located the young lover I had treated so badly. I was delighted—and greatly relieved—to find that he had put his life back together quite well without me, having graduated with a PhD in Somatic Psychology from the California College of Integral Studies, and now married to a loving, supportive man seventeen years older than I. He bore no ill will toward me, but was incredibly grateful to hear my apology. He also admitted his drinking and drug problems, though exacerbated by our relationship, had started and been brewing to the breaking point months before we had even met.

I lost track of Father Gabe Dunn as I had of Kurt Woolen, except for stray bits of information that found their way to me. Because most everyone still living in my hometown keeps up on the drama of everyone else's lives like a long-running afternoon soap opera, I heard Gabe had not been able to sustain the pressures of leading a parish, nor handle its myriad and less-than-religious administrative duties. He was now assigned to a rural contemplative monastery of aged nuns. It was a place of quiet prayer and modest acts of charity and tenderness that no doubt more gracefully fit Father Gabe's true nature. He also taught one class each semester at the local Catholic college. Students coming into independent adulthood, struggling to maintain the faith they were raised, sought him out and found him an empathetic sounding board. Another Oakford friend, a member of Alcoholics Anonymous, heard that Father Gabe attended all sorts of twelve-step meetings around town in the aftermath of losing his parish. Supposedly there was an addiction to opioids for pain he never articulated.

As ridiculous as it sounds, I feel oddly *betrayed* by Father Gabe leading Mass for Kurt Woolen. Who knows if he and Woolen became lifelong friends after high school during Gabe's seminary years and Woolen's prison ones, or if their paths had crossed once again sometime recently before Woolen's death? But somehow Father Gabe had become involved with those final Catholic rites and rituals that signify Kurt Woolen is, in fact, dead in body only, and that his essence, his soul, remains alive to know God for all eternity. There is even a promise of a greater forgiveness and compassion in his next life than I would ever allow him—or *he* ever allowed others—in this one.

The more and more I think about it—and as to why I obsessively keep turning it over in my mind I am totally dumbfounded and ignorant—the more I find it all utterly maddening. Contemplating Father Gabe's promiscuous offering of blessings and absolutions to Kurt Woolen's many sins *infuriates* me.

Until I saw his obituary, Woolen had not been in my thoughts for years, decades. And I am vehement with certainty that I had never been in his since the day he disappeared from English class right before our sophomore year ended. The rumor was he had flunked out, which was highly unlikely given the number of outright idiots who remained as students. More likely, his parents could no longer afford the moderate tuition given the multitude of offspring they were trying to educate in the Oakford Catholic school system. The realization dawns on me that whatever Father Gabe's eulogy of Kurt Woolen's life may be, it will not contain any single remembrance or recognition of me or of his violence against me. I am ridden with insult: *I* am not remembered.

One night, seven months after coming across Kurt Woolen's obituary, I encounter another one listed on *The Oakford Daily Journal* website. This one is a couple of weeks old. It is a much longer and more detailed obituary regarding the life of Father Gabriel Dunn.

It notes his extensive educational background, assorted parish assignments and chaplaincy at the monastic convent, and his expertise regarding the historical context of the gospel parables he enthusiastically shared as a professor at Oakford's Catholic college. His talent at guitar, the successful sobriety of nearly a decade, his great generosity and open heartedness to all people regardless of social standing are highlighted as well. All of this is followed by a long list of surviving siblings and deeply loved nephews and nieces. The obituary's only omission is his cause of death.

It is from a friend I contact the next day that I learn what most everyone in Oakford who read Father Gabe's obituary already knew—he killed himself. Placing a hunting rifle under his chin, he fired, not only blasting his brains from his skull, but also blowing off his handsome, gentle face with its soft eyes and shy, modest smile.

His body was discovered in his car by early Sunday morning golfers, parked in the course's lot where it was the lone vehicle when they arrived. The golf course, which housed the country club my drunken twenty-year high school reunion had been held, borders on a beautiful, lush state forest and bird preserve with much-walked hiking trails. Father Gabe had last been seen at the wedding he officiated the night before for a couple of former students. He had smiled and laughed and mingled at the reception, and there were several photos of him posed with the wedding party and different guests. He seemed his usual low-key, simple self. Saying he had to be up early the next morning to lead Mass for the faithful and good nuns of the monastery, he left around ten o'clock.

For several weeks after learning this, and compulsively rereading his online obituary, I am shadowed by a breaking sadness. It is the *loneliness* of Gabe's act that is so devastating, and the self-hate expressed by his violence against his own beautifully boyish, soulful face. It haunts me. All that was carried, locked away, unsaid, in his most private self. It is beyond my knowing, beyond my imagining. But what I can surmise of it, what I can push my heart to identify and understand, is crushing.

Images of his teenage naked body in the gym shower with its barely sprouted line of pubic hair around the thin, longish cock compete and intermingle in my mind's eye with images of his now adult body laid out uncovered on a coroner's table, his face shattered, disappeared. An old, elaborate fantasy of mine is reanimated, that of my very own life-correcting time machine. And this time that time machine takes me back to Gabe at our twenty-year high school reunion. This time I am outside my old adolescent desires and drunken plotting to seduce him. This time I can see and hear him as *him*. He can at last trust to say aloud all that he cannot say, dares not say, to any other person in his life in Oakford, Kentucky. He can say it all to me now because this time I am present to him at last. As he struggles in his hell of unspoken self and inwardly turned hate, of his endless loneliness, I will listen and care and love him without agenda.

I remember something I had forgotten about the last time we spent together at that high school reunion. I recall the full, accepting embrace as he said goodbye to me at the end of my alcohol-fueled confession. He did not linger or move his arms or hands anywhere else around my body during that embrace. There was no subjugated eroticism or unconscious sensuality. Just a brief but total holding close, a moment of authentic Christian brotherhood. Father Gabe Dunn was offering true friendship in that act of embrace. And I had not only minimized it but had thoroughly forgotten it in my contempt at having temporarily fallen back into the trap of Catholicism. Guilt enfolds me at my failure to realize and appreciate the grace, the *purity* of the grace, he so selflessly offered in that moment.

I spend a few days seized with the idea of making the long multiple-connecting flight to Kentucky. I want to stand at Gabe's gravesite in the Catholic cemetery right off the interstate highway on the outskirts of Oakford. The cemetery where my father, mother, brother, grandparents, and numerous other family, long-ago neighbors, teachers, and a couple of good friends who died when I was growing up, are all now buried. Perhaps there, in that vast, endless acreage of green silence, I might finally come to know what remains so unknown about the boy I first loved.

As the months pass, the impact of Gabe's suicide subsides to something more bearable, though at times it roils and strikes with an awful, destructive immediacy where I am again lost in its ceaseless, entangling unknowns. But as time goes on, a bizarre and incongruous thing also occurs. Something else comes back to awareness—a memory I haven't recalled since the event occurred in 1970, during the autumn semester.

Without the daily torment of Kurt Woolen and having worked all summer outdoors mowing the grass of the golf course and country club grounds where Father Gabe Dunn would take his life decades later, I was thriving during my junior year at Oakford Catholic High School in ways new and unexpected to me. I was clear skinned and tanned, taller, my hair growing out long onto my shoulders, and dressing in fashionable bell-bottom jeans and bold-colored paisley shirts bought with my own money. For the most part, I was now left alone by most bullies and rarely experienced any physical violence or threats of such from them. A tight, close circle of friends was coming together for me, my first ever in high school.

The only person who picked on me, who showed off by making fun of how I sounded and walked and dressed, calling me names, who hit me up against my head as hard as he could, was another football player. This one was a senior named Bobby Zogg. Like Kurt Woolen, he was rarely brought into the game as he had no speed nor as much strength compared to other boys on the team. Still, he had the swaggering-cock vanity that marked most of them. And, I must admit, he did have an imposing, muscular build that might have made him hot and attractive if he didn't also have such a sharp, squinty possum-like face and a real-deal redneck country boy "hee-haw" jackass laugh.

We were in the same Introduction to Film class taught by the young army wife of a soldier serving in Vietnam, Sheila Buckman, who could not have been more than five or six years older than the sixteen- and seventeen-year-olds she taught. She had lustrous waist-length brown hair and matching rich brown eyes, and she was dazzlingly beautiful to all of us. Especially to the straight boys who, when they were not making leering wolf faces behind her back, strutted up and smiled eagerly and stupidly trying to impress her.

Because I knew so much about the history of movies and film technique, and because I had already seen a number of the classic films referenced in the textbook, Mrs. Buckman lavished a lot of attention and praise on me, often deferring to my knowledge in her lessons to the class. She once told me privately that she thought I should be the one teaching it and was extremely impressed that I read Pauline Kael's weekly movie reviews in *The New Yorker* at the Oakford Public Library.

As it became more obvious that I was Mrs. Buckman's favored one, Bobby Zogg picked up the frequency and intensity of his undercutting verbal and physical attacks on me. Always out of eyesight of Mrs. Buckman, of course. One day during class, he said some cruel, taunting threat or pulled some stunt meant to demean me. The specifics have disappeared from memory. But out of my mouth, unplanned and unexpected—shocking me more than anyone else—I confronted him in a quaking, nervous voice that was still strong enough to be heard by everyone in the room, including Mrs. Buckman. "What's your problem? I haven't done anything to you. I don't bother you. Really, why do you act like this?" I asked.

Mrs. Buckman smiled quizzically, but amused, and said nothing. A few kids laughed, but most just looked at me looking straight at Bobby Zogg. It probably lasted thirty seconds, if even that long, but there was nothing but silence from him before he finally averted his face from mine.

As terrified as I was for the next few days, tense and alert, steeling myself for some violent revenge beating or degradation, Bobby Zogg did nothing. On occasion, he would look at me up and down with emphatic disgust and then turn away. I was fine with that.

I don't know why my moment of...what? Self-assertion? Courage? Just sheer "I'm fed-up and have had enough?" However named, it has not stood out or been recalled until the aftermath of Kurt Woolen's and Father Gabriel Dunn's dying. It has never been part of the repertoire of favorite stories I tell, much less something I have returned to proudly savor or draw inspiration. But somehow, it has resurrected in my consciousness after lying dormant for close to forty-five years.

It puzzles me that this significant moment of my first faltering step toward claiming myself has not been remembered, much less *treasured* enough, to become one of the key stories, if not the key story, that makes up my personal legend of self. This was the ending of my being a victim, with the promise to never again allow such mistreatment and violence against myself.

Remembering Bobby Zogg's flushed red face turning away from my gaze in that long chasm of fraught silence makes me feel happier than I have in months.

Though I still feel grief over Gabe's self-immolation, life slowly assumes proportion again. I can admit now Kurt Woolen's death upended me with the unpleasant truth that despite my hard-won knowledge there is no fairness in this life, I still harbored a profound desire that it did. It shocks me that I have held on to some hope that the old pain from my teenage years—a pain I self-destructively wallowed in during my twenties and much of my thirties—remained thirsting for some form of justice, something that would make all the physical and emotional traumas "healed" and "redeemed" in that stupid, fatuous Oprah Book Club way.

I thought I was at peace living with the scars. No longer hiding them but no longer scratching at them or, worse, highlighting them as certification and proof of my greater suffering and greater need, especially a greater need for love over everyone else's. But I had fooled myself into thinking that none of it *mattered* any longer or could ever be felt again in any meaningful or necessary way.

What mattered to Gabe, what he held so close for so long and could not contain within himself any longer, will remain an agonizing and sorrowful mystery to me. Even though we had not seen or spoken to each other in over twenty-five years, I hate so much that he suffered so viciously alone. But it is my great foolishness and vanity to think my fantasized return in his life could have "saved" him in any way. The unyielding ruthless truth that confronts me is I was as unimportant to Father Gabe Dunn as I was to Kurt Woolen. I thought I knew this all along and had accepted it when so obviously and painfully I had not. Gabe will always be the first boy I loved. I will always remember his sweetness, his constant and humble longing to always be good, to do good, no matter what demons and confusions, fears and loathing, coursed through him. But there is no escape from this cold, incontrovertible fact—I did not know him at all, and he never desired me to do so.

I will never visit Father Gabriel Dunn's grave. Most likely, I will never visit Oakford ever again. It has been six years since my last trip there, and in that time, the remaining aunts and uncles, at least the favorite ones, have now died. The cousin I am closest to and have the most fun with, I see every couple of years in Las Vegas or some Florida beach town where her family vacations. My two best friends from high school who made their lives in Oakford have children—and most significantly, grandchildren—in other states and are considering moving closer to them. And they are more likely to come visit me in San Francisco now that we are all fast approaching retirement.

As for Bobby Zogg, he married Jeannie Scott, a popular cheerleader free of the snobbery of most girls in her clique. I liked her. She was genuinely friendly, always chattering away good-naturedly and non-stop to everyone, even me, in her classes and at parties. A few years after graduating high school, I heard she filed for divorce, their short marriage having given them two children. The word was that he, like so many other Oakford high school football players of that era, now in young adulthood and bereft of his standing among a team, was a raging alcoholic.

I don't know anything of what happened to him after that. I don't know if he ever remarried or got sober or is still living in Oakford. I couldn't care less, frankly. But perhaps I will find out some day. Perhaps while reading the online edition of my old hometown's newspaper, I will run across his obituary and think of him again for the first time in many years.

# Andrew

It is an early December morning, and I am in a bed in a home that is not my own. Andrew, so beautiful in ways that I am not, and who has no claim—indeed, even less claim than I—on this bed and this home, has gotten up, nude, from underneath the heavy gold comforter, and now stands. The barest sunlight of a cold dawn seeps through the drawn white curtains.

"What's going on?" I ask, sleepily rousing to awareness.

"I think I should leave early today," Andrew says. "I've been missing too many classes."

"And your exams must be soon," I respond, wanting to show that I understand, am sympathetic.

"Right," he answers matter-of-factly. But Andrew does not move, does not grab his red-and-blue Diesel underwear trunks from the floor.

Lying on my right side facing him, I open and then shut my eyes with the craving to sleep. I pull the comforter up to my neck.

"Andrew," I whisper with effort, my eyes shut, "is everything okay?"

"Sure," he replies. "I just want to look at you."

I smile to myself; I force my eyes open and smile at him. The tenuous light through the window places Andrew in silhouette, and he seems larger, more muscular, with limbs long and lithe, and graceful too. Almost a sculpture.

Andrew brings one hand to his right nipple as the other languidly slides down his stomach to touch his lengthening penis.

"Oh, Andrew," I say in as friendly a tone as I can at this hour, "it's too early." Amused as I am at his almost constantly erect and ready twenty-three-year-old cock, I shut my eyes again and roll over, my back to him.

"I want to make sure I don't forget you." His voice cracks as if he is going to cry.

I turn back quickly, alarmed, though not quite sure what I am hearing or comprehending. Andrew smiles at me, that crooked, rascally smile that unlocks parts of me despite myself. But he's cloaked in a shroud of sadness that is so unlike him. He begins to masturbate with one hand clutching his fully thickened cock, the palm of his other hand rubbing its head in circular motions.

"I love you, Sammie," he whispers with quiet urgency.

Another lock that only Andrew can open. No one else has permission to call me Sammie ever. I am always Samuel. Instinctively, I reach out to him.

But he backs away, shaking his head no. He lets loose of his fat stiff member, now pointing outward, an arrow aimed ready to pierce my resistance of flesh, of heart.

Even though the temperature-controlled room is warm, I am aware of the deep winter chill sneaking near the window. The sun is brighter, and glimpses of it strike Andrew's body as he stretches, arms upward and torso curving as if in a pagan dance of worship. The sensuous line of him that flashes in the bedroom sun and shadows stuns me.

Drinking in the sight of him, I hold my breath. I feel invaded by his beauty. Almost disturbed by it, even as I hunger for it.

Andrew puts two fingers between his soft pronounced lips and wets them heavily. He rubs them across his nipples, which he then pinches to the point of shuddering pain. He begins to stroke faster, occasionally rubbing the cock head in a circular motion against his palm. He moans as if wounded.

I feel absorbed into his skin as I watch the muscles on his chest and in his arms ripple, repose, then move again in steady grace. Hints of the rising sun continue to slash on and off him. Despite my own erection and lusts now arising, I am still and do not grip my own penis. To do so would be to break the spell cast by our now locked eyes.

Andrew makes small yelps as he journeys closer to climax. He continues to stroke and rub, but I know he is also trying to hold back, refusing to give up this moment where we are so transfixed upon each other.

He falls to his knees screaming, "Sammie! Sammie!" an unholy growl of yearning and anger as orgasm overtakes him. Two jetting arcs soar out of his body, followed by two shorter but equally intense ejaculations. Andrew shakes violently on the bedroom floor, possessed, waiting for it to subside.

As his breathing returns to normal, he brings his knees up against his chest and places his arms around them, rocking slow and quiet. Then, at last, he begins to cry, releasing the burden of tears he most likely has wanted to shed since waking.

I jump out of bed, also naked. I go to him, coming down to the floor, and pull him close to me, holding him tightly and tenderly in the silence. The sun is at full radiance through the curtains, but the chill in the air lingers.

"I love you, Sammie," he says. "I give you things for free that I never give other people, even for money."

I am gentle. "That doesn't necessarily mean it's love."

"Yes, it does," Andrew delicately volleys back.

We do not talk anymore. His head against my chest, I comfort him as if he were a child hurt and confused in his first experience of life's unfairness. We lose track of time, but eventually I get us off the floor by telling him to go take a shower while I make breakfast. He won't be leaving as early as planned.

We eat in silence except for a soft, shapeless comment thanking me for making his favorite pancakes. Strawberry.

Before he leaves, I broach the subject, saying that perhaps his continuing to see clients is "starting to take a toll, what with school and all." And even though I have no idea of any specifics, I find myself coming out with these words: "I'm sure we can find other ways for you to get through school."

"No, it's nothing like that," Andrew sighs, though I am unconvinced. He gives me a sustained hug goodbye, putting all his strength into it.

For the first time in the four months I have known him, I stand outside on the extended front driveway to see him off, bundled against the cutting winter air in a luxury bathrobe that is not mine. I watch until his dented, scratched gray Accord of many years reaches the driveway's end and takes a left, vanishing onto the road outside the estate's enclosing stone walls.

I found Andrew through a now-defunct website where college and graduate students advertise their massage skills and erotic company. The wealthier clients I house-sit for often leave extra-large wads of cash for emergencies involving their ridiculously pampered pets or some unexpected maintenance crisis. They tell me to keep the money if it turns out to be unnecessary. So, I indulge myself in escorts. It's more efficient and less emotionally taxing than investing in a "real" relationship.

In our initial meeting, Andrew was very polite, almost impersonal, speaking in brief declarative sentences that gave little room for conversation. But I sensed right off that he was not as confident nor as removed as he pretended. A low pulsating uncertainty, even slight fear, exuded from underneath his pose. The barely perceptible droop of his posture and his looping, clumsy walk gave him away, as did the searching eagerness of his green eyes. These would normally be red flags warning me not to go through with it. Or, at the very least, not invite a return engagement. Inexplicably, there was something about his false front of cool bravado that I found charming and even poignant. I immediately liked him.

Once we were naked and in bed, however, he revealed other, unpredicted aspects of himself. His innate vulnerability was still present, but there was also an essential, keener piece of his being claimed through sex. Which inspired me in ways I had not been inspired in many years. We instantaneously discovered we were matched in sex in a way that is rare, easing into both uninhibited play and near-feral lust, communicating emotions fierce and sensitive that have no other language or means of articulation except through bodies meeting, joining, and moving in their own experimenting, discovering rhythms. We were intuitively free, without thought or care, from the usual strict roles as to who was "top" or "bottom," "butch" or "femme," "dominant" or "submissive." We simply followed our desires as they arose in the moment.

We were not without the awkwardness of off-timed, misread cues, missed kisses, colliding elbows and knees, or of uneasy, strained positioning—all the customary clumsiness of first-time sex. But there was something vibrating in Andrew's appetite that resonated with me, that brought out feelings I had long given up and buried. There was no act in him. A cardinal element of himself was exposed and shared in how he used his mouth and hands, his fingers and tongue, his ass and cock. And in how he responded to mine. Sex expressed his most fundamental person, and there was no hesitation or timidity in it at all— only happy carnality and hedonism.

As for myself, I had been so desert dry of passion and joy that I could no longer remember if I had ever actually known them. Perhaps they were only imaginary threads woven into a now-frayed tapestry, one memorializing a love that had never truly existed. It was unintentional, even unwanted, to have this private sphere revived after so many years.

He stayed considerably past the time planned for our first night, and only asked payment for the originally scheduled two hours. Ever cautious, I paid him the full amount for the total time we spent with one another.

During our next two evenings together, we took turns preparing dinner—an elaborate arrangement of sushi and sashimi delicacies from me, tomato soup and grilled cheese sandwiches from him. I came to know him better without having to reveal too much of myself. Andrew chatted enthusiastically about all he was learning in one of his business classes on the arcane workings of the stock market (which remains beyond my understanding to this day). I shared with him what turned out to be useful information and insights on Joyce's "The Dead" and O'Connor's "A Good Man is Hard to Find" that he incorporated into a midterm paper for his "boring" literature course. He received an 'A' for his work. I was pleased beyond reason.

On our fourth date, I stopped pretending to be the owner of the estate that belonged to an airline executive and his heiress wife currently on an around-the-world second honeymoon. He had already guessed as much. He, in turn, stopped charging me.

I usually meet Andrew on Sundays after he has kept his weekend round of appointments. He appears right before noon, soon after checkout time at the expensive hotels or cheap motels he passes his Saturday night. He always has a bounty of stories about the men he has spent his time.

Except for the rare restaurant or movie, we never go outside the estate. It seems to provide an oasis for him, not only from his work but from campus life as well. One recent Sunday afternoon, I peered over the book I was reading, observing him in studious concentration as he wrestled with complicated statistical formulas for his Advanced Economic Theory class. It registered with me that we had become comfortable sharing silence.

Andrew has begun arriving earlier, even sometimes on Saturday afternoons. It is also becoming his habit to make the two-hour drive from his small college town in southern Illinois here to St. Louis during the middle of the week without the justification of a client appointment. As he did last night.

Now that he has gone, I fight the urge to masturbate, images of his earlier sexual act branded into memory, taunting and tempting me.

But I take a quick shower and then dress, abandoning my morning rituals. The disheveled kitchen and the unmade bed will wait. For some perversity I am in no mood to analyze, I leave Andrew's staining come unattended on the bedroom carpet.

I have no plans beyond my daily nebulous promise to "do some work" on one of my rarely published poems. But that task feels suddenly and particularly claustrophobic. I find myself agitated, not wanting to be confined alone in the house for the rest of the day, waiting until the dark of early evening, so I can then call Andrew and see how he is now feeling. It is my rule that we never text or email.

Since my traveling employers' idiotically expensive XTS silver Cadillac has sat parked in their six-car garage the last ten days, I decide to drive into the city. I feel compelled to go to its old gay neighborhood, the once-trendy Central West End near Forest Park. It is early enough in the day for only a few serious shoppers to be out, so there should be a less hostile and competitive holiday crowd.

I've not thought about what to buy Andrew as a Christmas gift. Knowing that we are entwined enough for such a symbol to pass between us, I nevertheless have been reluctant to give it recognition. Today, though, it feels important, imperative even, that I do so. Window-shopping, I wander inside three stores to browse lovely hand-painted Christmas cards with enticing pastoral settings. At a fourth, I price exquisitely woven Italian sweaters, even though I know they are far outside any range I can afford.

We have not discussed any Christmas plans or rituals between us, partly because Christmas does not mean the same thing to me that it does to so many other people. I am in no way religious, and I have no family. Besides, the heiress wife expects me to spend the season at the estate while she and her husband ski some exclusive retreat in Switzerland. Andrew, I assume, will make time for his mother, her fourth husband, and his younger half-sister in Oak Park outside of Chicago. Nevertheless, I feel pangs of an odd nostalgia for a holiday morning with him that we have never experienced.

I stand in the center of a compact, cramped men's boutique with shiny, slick hardwood floors. The music is a generic house beat throbbing across the room, that eternally tiresome synthesized rhythm that has propelled far too many desperate, drunken dramas on Saturday nights in gay bars and dance clubs for God knows how many generations. Unfolding a handsome and unjustly priced white wool sweater with large wood buttons up the neck—a style Andrew has never worn, but I know would look spectacular on him—I realize how very little I know of Andrew at all.

He talks about his classes, and he loves to recount his abundant sexual exploits on campus. Andrew is an unapologetic sensualist who scopes out opportunities for sex throughout the week in the dormitory where he lives, assorted study areas in the student center and library, and the campus gym's sauna and steam room where he refuses to drape himself in the customary towel.

Beyond this, however, practically no other details of his life as a student are familiar to me. I don't even know if he has friends his own age, buddies he goes drinking with or spends in late night talks about their ambitions and futures or the meaning of life. I don't know about any places he goes to just for fun to hang out or if he attends ball games and other sporting events or partakes in anything on offer at the university such as guest speakers or concerts or plays. Beyond swimming and some weightlifting, I have no idea of how he fills his free time.

It occurs to me, for the first time strangely enough, that between his classes, his clients, and me, Andrew does not have much of the typical life of a college undergraduate at all. I start to feel a great heartache for him, almost a mourning.

"See anything you like?" a silly, airy voice intrudes.

A very tall, almost anorexic-looking young man stands across the sweater shelf, batting his teasing brown eyes at me. He has a close-to-the-skull razor cut allocating one narrow strip of verdant black hair atop his head. Dressed in a perfectly tailored suit of subtle gray with a pink-and-black-checkered shirt and bold yellow yolk bowtie, the clothing and colors somehow blend remarkably well.

His likability makes me smile. "No, thank you. My mind is off on Jupiter," I nervously laugh.

He laughs back. "Oooooo. Drugs? Or boyfriend drama?" he asks ardently. Despite the almost comic lilt of his high-camp speech, he is genuinely interested.

I look at him, hesitate, then stammer out, "I think...I don't really know...I guess...maybe it is...the latter." I trail off in a nervous, self-deprecating laugh. "I'm too old to be playing Annie Hall," I quip.

"Who's Annie Hall?" he quips back, playfully raising his finely waxed left eyebrow.

My laughter is now real, as is his. Then we stand there dawdling, unsure what to say next. We smile at each other. I swiftly become nervous again.

"Well, I better get going," I offer as I ineptly attempt to fold the sweater back into perfect form.

"Here. I'll do that," he says, stretching his arm across the pile of tasteful, costly sweaters. His fingers lightly graze my hand with insinuating touch.

"Thank you," I gulp, struck bashful and uneasy. While I have no sexual interest at all in the clerk, I am startled that he has displayed such attraction toward me. It is unusual for someone else to initiate physical contact, and I am always disconcerted by it. I nod my head in modest acknowledgement before abruptly turning to exit the store.

"Please. Do take good care of your good self," he declares, his floating pitch rising comically again. But he speaks without affectation; there is seriousness and concern in his tone.

The street outside now buzzes with more activity. People hurry with purposeful steps. I feel an instant lightheadedness. Despite my earlier heavy breakfast, I am unexpectedly hungry. I begin the walk up several blocks to a favorite cafe, the wind's chill reviving me enough to keep me moving.

There's no denying I am selfish with Andrew, I think to myself. I knew from the first time I laid eyes on him that he could upend my life. I did not—still do not?—want that.

In my twenties, I had moved in with a fellow graduate student, both of us in a great rush for the defining grand romance of our lifetimes. We also wanted to approximate a domesticity for ourselves that we desperately hoped would conjure stability and banish all anxiety and doubt about our future, our meaning, as a couple. Though we both knew it was right to end it five years later, the failure of it knifed my heart.

But it was a love affair soon after the relationship ended that baked me into the personality and its attendant habits I now clung to with such ferocity. I think I went slightly insane during it. He was married and closeted, a narcissistic politician with fetishes I would indulge even as they became boring and repetitious, petty, to me. I hated who I became—weak and womanly in the worst way, at least "womanly" in that old sense of losing myself totally to a man, defining my happiness by his, willingly and resentfully giving up my identity and self-sufficiency to him. Martyring myself to his entitled and oblivious selfishness.

Love then had meant all-consuming passion and endless tears, sick exhaustion, relentless need. I was out control with delusional hope and tumultuous grief over what could not, would not, ever be. He had no compunction ending it, cold and efficient, when I finally attempted minor, half-hearted rebellions of independence.

Even more than publishing another volume of poems, my primary commitment has been to never give myself over to anyone again who might inspire such burning, absurd self-annihilation.

Now on the cusp of forty, I have allowed Andrew into my life. And it is thoughts of Andrew that uncomfortably gnaw at me, propelling my walk to what now seems the safe harbor of the cafe.

At last, I arrive. Its once chic, then out of fashion, and perhaps now once again on-trend exposed brick walls are filled with massive canvasses of manic bold colors and shapes that irritate me. I take a seat at the battered wood table looking out onto the street. My ordinary preference is to sit in less conspicuous public spots. But today I crave more of the sunlight beaming through the huge sheer glass window.

A dark-haired, smooth-shaved waiter with conventional good looks, not much older than Andrew, takes my order of a glass of wine and a salad with lean strips of chicken breast and assorted greens. I catch the wet spicy scent of his pungent cologne when he gingerly leans over to place the food in front of me and refill the wine glass I too rapidly drained.

Andrew had known four fathers. His biological one abandoned him when he was only two years old, leaving his nineteen-year-old-mother to raise him alone. Last summer, before we had come to be in each other's lives, Andrew met him. "Short and bald and fat and angel-faced. A lot like some of my nicer clients," was the description Andrew gave. He had obviously inherited the father's shortness and angel face but staved off—at least for the present—the baldness and fat, having a full shock of straw-colored hair and a lean compact body he strained to define and make larger at the campus gym.

"He wasn't at all what I had pictured," Andrew said. "But that's alright. I could see me in his eyes." It is unlikely they will ever see each other again.

Andrew has never once requested to role play "daddy/boy" or "father/son" fantasies in our sex. I am grateful for that.

His second father (Andrew never referred to any of the other men who married his mother as "stepfather") was a friendly, affectionate old man, more granddad than dad, who generously indulged all of Andrew's passing interests and enthusiasms as a very young child, giving him pets and buying him sports equipment and musical instruments, amused by and encouraging of his many curiosities. But he became serious, even stern, when Andrew started school, impressing upon him that "education is the key to everything in life" and patiently helped him with his homework whenever he could. He died soon after Andrew turned ten.

He only shared one story about his third father—the terrorizing experience of that father wildly pointing a loaded gun back-and-forth between Andrew, his mother, and his new baby sister while screaming they had all destroyed his life.

Mercifully, the fourth father was a healthier, more stable man who never had anything in common with Andrew. They were strangers, albeit friendly and respectful ones.

Andrew's decision to have sex with men for money was made without hesitation and much practicality. "I don't want to be stuck with student loans for the rest of my life. Besides," he grinned, "I like sex a lot. Why not get paid for it? And when you get down to it, it's more of an education, at least about some things, than I'll ever learn from going to school."

I picture him laying across the bed in a countryside mobile home as an unhappy, lumpy-fleshed high school history teacher, ungraded papers strewn about, gives him a blow job after strapping his bare buttocks with a leather belt. And I recall Andrew's engagement with a retired widowed doctor in his early seventies, "quite distinguished looking," Andrew noted, who had him lean over an examining table naked in his study, pretending to be a high school athlete being given a physical. He said it had felt "very, very weird," but cheerfully had to admit, "it also gave me the most rock-hard boner I've ever had in my life."

"The nicest one, but kind of sad," is how Andrew described his favorite client. A man only a couple of years older than me who was the deacon of some obscure small church in some obscure small town on the way to St. Louis. "His wife went on a religious retreat once a year and this was the only time he ever had sex with a guy. He saved up for it in secret for a long time, like a kid does for a special toy his parents won't buy for him, but he just has to have. We kiss and jerk off, and that's all he wants, and it makes him so happy."

I try to leap inside Andrew's mind, his eyes, his *skin*, try to see what he must see, must be taking in and moved by in these scenes in which he is the most crucial, most needed actor.

Something rises high from my heart, engulfing me. I ache to be with him again, both of us naked under the thick gold comforter, holding his head to my chest in the darkest of night, my heartbeat a signal to him that he is loved, he is loved, he is loved.

With a jolt of surprise, I become aware of the waiter standing to my left, his crotch disconcertingly close to my face. He looks down on me with a peeved frown. "Is there anything wrong, sir?"

"No," my voice quivers. I am hotly embarrassed. I have shed a few discernible tears without knowing I was doing so.

Jokes should be made at my expense for such public foolishness. But it is apparent that Andrew's presence in my life cannot be laughed away. The puny wry "wit" of ironic detachment will not be enough strategy to shield me this time.

I pay my bill and walk briskly out of the cafe. I stride down the street, searching for a popular bakery I know is nearby. I need to inhale fresh bread and baking cookies, childhood Christmas smells.

The snapping cold air feels almost attacking. And the sun is too dazzlingly bright. I stop on the sidewalk and look around, worried I have gone past the bakery by a couple of blocks, worried that it may no longer exist. Another wave of light-headedness strikes me. But I know with certainty the two hastily swallowed glasses of wine cannot be blamed.

I am penetrated by the image of Andrew, the sun seizing then losing his naked body in its morning light, highlighting, even sanctifying, his beauty. His falling to his knees as he ejaculates wildly, crying out, "Sammie. Sammie." The incantation he made of my name is now heard as an anguished demand.

Turning in the opposite direction, my pace quickens with every step. Panic shoots through me. The possibility now seems to exist that I won't ever see him again.

Andrew has insisted he be seen. Seen in all the ways that I have not been open to, beyond the boundaries and rules I have set up to keep him at bay, to prevent him from burrowing into my fortressed heart. This morning Andrew made manifest the inescapable fact—he exists *outside* me. I must see him as he is in himself, or else I will lose him.

I bypass the bakery once more, but this time I am aware of doing so. The bountiful aroma of warm rising dough wafts onto the street. It rallies hope within me.

Returning to the car, I sit. My heart races to the point of almost hurting, so unbearable is the fear of never seeing Andrew again. I command myself to breathe slowly, willing my heart and mind to peace.

Calm now and fully sober, I start the engine and begin the drive back to the estate. But on my way there, I spy an approaching off-ramp and veer right. Thoughtfully and steadily accelerating the speed, but keeping within the limit, I travel this unfamiliar road that will take me to Andrew.

# The Boy in the Audience

He has lied to be here. His mom believes he is at the library studying for a calculus test this coming Monday. But she (and his dad) also believe he will be attending the University of Kentucky after his high school senior year, though he has even less interest in the University of Kentucky than he does calculus. Unbeknownst to anyone except his best friend Jamie, his plan is to leave for New York City the day after graduation to begin his career—no, his *vocation*—as a playwright.

He understands it will be a long, arduous struggle to get his first play on Broadway. His idol Tennessee William did not do so until he was thirty-four-years-old with *The Glass Menagerie*. But he will not allow himself to be detoured as Williams was by a dead-end, low-paying job in a shoe factory and years bouncing between universities. *He* would get to New York City the second the meaningless high school diploma was in his hand a year-and-a-half from now, find his way into the off-Broadway theatre scene, and after two or three productions will write the play that propels him onto a Broadway stage. He figures it should take five years, seven at most, to accomplish this.

So as not to be too noticeable, he sits in the side right section of the movie theater a good five seats in from the aisle, practically to the wall, rather than his usual place among the rows in the center. Of the dozen or so of the audience that he can see from his vantage point, he realizes all are men. And all of them are alone. He doesn't dare turn around to survey those who are sitting behind him in the back rows, but he intuitively knows those who do are also men, and alone as well.

It is difficult to make out faces as everyone sits waiting for the first showing of the day. The previews haven't started yet, but light is projected as local ads pop up on the screen, running in a loop. They're the same static, unmoving photographs with slogans and addresses that have been showing the last three years—advertisements for a used car lot, the local dairy company, the town's most prominent bank, a barbeque restaurant, etc. He catches side profiles of faces but is mostly confronted with backs. By the profiles, and such clues as posture and haircuts, he deduces most are college age or in their thirties, although there are two who look older (like his father's age) and one other who looks even older than them.

But no one else, except himself, looks like they are still in high school.

The movie he has snuck away to see is *The Boys in the Band*. It has made its way to his small Southern town several months after first being released in New York and shown throughout most of the country. So now on a damp, chilly Saturday afternoon in January 1971, the film which premiered in March of 1970, is finally here in Owensboro, Kentucky. It was barely advertised in the local newspaper, slotted in for a quick five-day run before the opening of *Patton* next Wednesday.

He is fully aware what the movie is about, of course, having read lots of reviews in magazines and newspapers like *The New Yorker*, *Holiday*, *Saturday Review*, and *Village Voice* which can only be found at the public library. Six months earlier, while thumbing through paperback books at the drugstore, he spotted the cover of the Dell edition. The image was the same as the movie's poster—all nine characters in black turtlenecks.

Fearful as he was, he hadn't hesitated to buy it. He knew the cashier would never register that eight of those men on the cover were homosexuals and that the ninth might well be one too. After all, they looked like ordinary guys, guys who could easily be part of a musical band. Obviously, not a current rock band, but more like a jazz band of the 1950s. That would be the cashier's assumption regarding the title and cover if he even paid that much attention to his purchase.

He has read the paperback of the play script three times, and often picks it up to read a scene or two, and sometimes only a brief exchange of dialogue. At this point, he's practically got it memorized.

When he first walked into the movie theater—the theater he has been going to all his life since *The Ten Commandments* at age five in 1959 (that's how long it sometimes took for the biggest movies to come to Owensboro)—he had gone into the men's restroom. Now his usual routine is to go to the restroom before he takes his seat anyway; it's a habit instilled in him by his dad years ago, most likely at that introduction to moviegoing with *The Ten Commandments*. But his mind was burning with the thought that perhaps today someone might be in there waiting for him. From one of the half-dozen books about human sexuality he has surreptitiously read at the library, he learned homosexual men "cruise" each other in restrooms, standing at a urinal pretending to piss until another man comes up to the one next to it. If both are interested in sex, one will strike up a casual conversation as they linger there. Sometimes they will glance at the other's dick. And sometimes even begin stroking their own, getting hard.

Such a scenario terrifies him. But this is the encounter he *must* have if he is to be prepared for life in New York.

As is his luck whenever he does screw up enough courage to risk the next step, nothing happened. No one was there at the other urinal, cock displayed, waiting for him. So, he did what he had been taught and peed before the movie started. But he did not immediately zip back up. Instead, he stared at the door, trying to will someone into walking through it.

He stood there waiting for what seemed an extremely long time, his dick hanging out. But he did not get hard. It had been both a blessing and a curse that in the showers of freshman year PE he was so anxious and afraid about getting a boner in the middle of all his naked classmates, his long, skinny dick would instead shrink up and turtle inside the folds of the shaft's skin. It looked as if he were uncircumcised. He was mocked for this and deeply ashamed, but he knew the mocking would have been far worse, if not violent, had it moved in the opposite direction.

Feeling foolish, he placed his dangling member back into his underwear. He laughed to himself as he washed his hands, remembering he had seen Walt Disney's *Pollyanna* at this exact same theater when he was six years old. Now, ten years later, he's standing in the restroom with his cock out. But it was a rueful laugh. Had anyone actually come in, he knows he probably would have bolted away in a panic, too scared to have done anything at all.

He accepts what he is but remains muddy and inexact as to what he can do about it. Books on human sexuality in the library, even the more up-to-date ones, only take his understanding so far in how to navigate it all. Fiction has been more helpful to his imagination and sense of possibility. He had read *Portnoy's Complaint* a year earlier and was immensely reassured that his own crazy, constant, and immersive masturbation was shared at least by Alex Portnoy, even if the source of their sexual hungers diverged. It had made a dent against the guilt over his own maddening lust by making him laugh at it. *Myra*

*Breckinridge*—the book, not the movie, as the movie had not and would not ever play in a theater, even at the drive-ins, of Baptist and Catholic-dominated Owensboro—had confused him. It took him a while to understand what a "dildo" was and how it could be used. The description of stripped, hunky Rusty bent over and tied to a medical exam table had excited him thoroughly, but there was something hateful in the scene he couldn't relate to. He found a far greater erotic ideal in the other Gore Vidal novel he had read, *Washington, D.C.*, with its scene of two naked teenage boys lying on the bathroom floor as one jerks off the other, giving him his first ejaculation. That, to him, is the most desired frame of sex he wants to enter— a familiar act, playful and exciting, with a close friend his own age, each attracted to the other.

The string of "Coming Attractions" are played—the upcoming *Patton;* a new Elliot Gould movie he hasn't heard of called *Move*; a western titled *One More Train to Rob* with George Peppard; *The Owl and the Pussycat*, starring the mesmerizing Barbra Streisand whom he adores; and the most talked about movie of the moment, *Love Story*, with beautiful, golden-haired Ryan O'Neal.

At last, *The Boys in the Band* begins.

He is surprised by the bouncy, catchy opening credits with the song "Anything Goes" playing in the background. He understands the story will become more dramatic as it goes on but hadn't anticipated there might be spaces for such a light spirit. And he is captivated, *besotted*, with all he sees of New York and the different "boys" as they move about it. He loves Michael's apartment with its staircase to a second floor with a small skylight and a tiny, narrow hall leading to one bedroom and an adjoining bath. He loves even more how the kitchen opens onto a patio that, unlike every patio he has ever seen, is not on the ground with a lawn stretching out before it but is instead a rooftop overlooking the city.

There is so much to take in: he is fascinated by the different good-looking hustlers lined up on the street, lasciviously meeting Emory's coy glances; Donald's extra tipping of the gorgeous young blond parking lot attendant; the men of all ages and types that cheerfully pack the gay bar Hank meets Larry. He identifies with Donald's absorption in books, Emory's sissiness (though much relieved that his is not such a flaming extreme), Michael's restlessness and dissatisfaction. There is a glimpse of Donald's naked butt as he slides into the shower. The athletic Hank sweats away playing basketball, looking so much like a regular guy. Larry's easy, comfortable mix of masculinity, handsomeness, stylish fashion, and full enjoyment of Emory's campiness is a combination he's never seen in a man. The revelatory Bernard makes him aware that someone

Black can also be gay, something so obvious and logical, yet still an idea he never considered until he read about the movie in reviews.

And best of all, there is the dancing. The happiness he feels watching the boys form a chorus line to Martha and the Vandellas' "Heat Wave" is exhilarating. Their camaraderie, their *joy*! Theirs is the world he yearns to join.

He is the only one in the audience who laughs out loud when Michael proclaims, "There's one thing to say about masturbation: you certainly don't have to look your best." He doesn't think anything of it, but the second time he laughs aloud and alone (as Donald responds to Michael's "there was a time in my life I didn't go around announcing I was a faggot" with "that must have been before speech replaced sign language") he is momentarily embarrassed and feels somehow wrong. Later, long after the film is over and he gives it considerable thought, it dawns on him that as an audience they never became as one. Instead, each was an audience only of himself, privately focused on whatever character, situation, or monologue involved and confronted them personally. To publicly give away any sign of self-identification of the personal chords being struck or of the emotions provoked, even—perhaps *especially*—the pleasure of laughter over jokes with a decidedly homosexual flavor, was to risk a self-exposure they could not afford even in the relative anonymity of a movie theater.

The part of him that studies playwriting admires the timing of Alan's unexpected arrival at the birthday party. The author Mart Crowley grasps exactly when and how to "raise the stakes," a phrase he has taken to heart as the key to his own writing efforts. New tensions are set off within Michael and in the dynamic among the other guests due to the inconvenient presence of straight, married, socially rigid Alan.

He is thrown by his failure to fully appreciate the words as he read them on the page from how they could be so different when played out. There are more layers and textures revealed in their enactment. Michael's rising resentment of Alan, of having to accommodate Alan's beliefs and attitudes, of having to listen to his judgments of Emory, of having to behave differently—*to not be himself*—all because of Alan's being there. He stiffens his back. He lowers the register of his voice, and speaks more carefully, defensively. A steely deliberation in his tone emerges, however, as he subtly pushes back against Alan's condescending evasions that allude to, but at no point directly acknowledge Michael's homosexuality. In his readings of the script, he thought he understood Michael's painful self-hatred and self-destructiveness. But for the first time he appreciates that Michael's rage over what heterosexual Alan represents, what heterosexual Alan *requires*, is a crucial factor, maybe the most crucial factor, fueling all the rest.

Stakes rise once more as Harold ultimately makes his entrance into the birthday party being held in his honor. There is a new illicit thrill of New York City gay life to witness—Harold is smoking pot and offers it to the party, some of them taking hits. And the "Midnight Cowboy" hustler, Emory's gift, kisses Harold on the mouth. It is the first male kiss he has ever seen. As hasty and unromantic as it is presented, it still amazes him, making real something he often fears as far away, and perhaps impossible, to ever experience himself.

The interplay of bitchy insults between Michael and Harold, cutting with cold, sharp honesty, unnerves him. He and Jamie sometimes act this way when they are alone together, their good-natured bantering of one-upmanship becoming mean and bitter, wanting to make the other feel low and miserable, and them ending up almost hating each other. Yet it is obvious Michael and Harold are friends who hold a deep connection beyond their volley of hostilities. Michael nervously anticipates Harold's reaction as he opens the birthday gift he has created, and Harold is genuinely moved by the silver-framed photo of Michael with its personal inscription. It's an intimacy that Harold won't share with the rest of the group. Despite their many cruel remarks, they know and understand each other as no one else in the world does. It bonds them, and they care for each other in their own way, just as he and Jamie do.

Though these thoughts drift in and out as he watches *The Boys in the Band*, he is always and completely absorbed by it, missing nothing. He feels as if he is *inside* the movie, a guest at the party sitting unnoticed in the background. Silently observing, taking it all in, a part of and apart from the scene before him.

There is another moment of dancing, but this time it is a slow one to the sensual horns of "The Look of Love." The camera moves in close as Bernard holds Emory tight, and Emory leans his head against Bernard's body. He feels tears well up. Physical tenderness between two men is something else he has never seen before in his life.

The story progresses to its final phase: the vicious phone game Michael devises where everyone must call the one person they have truly loved and then unequivocally proclaim that love to them. The almost diametrically different Donald and Harold are the only ones who reject participating in the game. Whatever their neuroses and problems, they possess a core of self-respect they won't sacrifice. He admires them, sees that they are right in their choice, and knows he himself would jump at the chance to play this game if he could.

Who would he call? Someone who doesn't remember him. Who barely noticed him. Someone he didn't even talk to and who never talked to him. Someone without a name. So, someone who's telephone number he would never be able to find. But it is someone real. Four years earlier, as a twelve-year-old paperboy delivering the Sunday Louisville *Courier-Journal* with its fat multiple sections of news, sports, business, arts (with giant movie ads that on occasion take up a quarter of a page), colored comic strips, and a weekly Kentucky-themed magazine—a *big city* newspaper—he had met his one true love once and only once. He has never forgotten him.

It was a little after 7:00 a.m. in one of the two men's dormitories of Kentucky Wesleyan College, a small, private Methodist school founded in the 1850s as a training seminary for ministers. It is now far more secular and noted for its liberal arts and science programs. He was making his way down the fourth-floor hallway to leave that Sunday's paper in front of the last door on the left. But from the room directly across it, a student came out and began walking toward him, probably to the toilets and showers. He was stark naked. Stunned, knowing he couldn't turn and run away—and, of course, not wanting to since his curiosity was stronger than the shame about his curiosity—he kept walking toward the hypnotic naked body.

What leaves a forever mark he returns to over and over again is that the drowsy young man with disheveled hair—taller by a good three or four inches, well-proportioned, strong, lithe, with a forest of black pubic hair surrounding a sizeable thick dick—gives him a big, dumb grin and a wink as they pass each other, and says, "Hey, buddy!"

For several Sundays afterward, he made sure he was on the fourth floor of the dorm at 7:00 a.m. on the dot. Around week four, after not running into the winking, naked student again, he waits at the staircase for five, then ten minutes, hoping he will show up. He alters his delivery route so he can come as early as 6:30 a.m. After more weeks of no sightings, he arrives as late as 7:30 a.m. But no one, naked or clothed, ever stirs that early in the fourth-floor hallway again.

Still, this sexy man with the sleepy dumb grin, perfect body, flawless skin, large cock, and winking, welcoming "Hey, buddy!" has become his best friend with whom he tells everything. When he is lonely and hopeless, when the verbal taunts of other boys become unbearable and turn into pushing and slapping and hitting (once kicking him so hard in the balls he nearly vomited and passed out), this is the friend he conjures in imagination who allows him to cry about the injustice and pain of it all. The college student is also who he shares all his passionate dreams about the plan to leave Owensboro for a life of love and theatrical success in New York City. He has been with him through everything these last four years. He is his anchor, his savior. The one person he can reveal himself. In his fantasies of their conversations, they both are always naked, and he is always held by him.

If ever he were to see him again in real life, no matter how difficult it would be to say the words, he would, like Emory with his great crush Dr. Delbert Botts, DDS, ask the college boy from that long ago Sunday morning to please be his friend.

The characters he is most drawn to, perhaps because they are the ones most unlike him, are Hank and Larry. They take center stage during their turn in the phone game, bringing to the surface the jealousies and conflicts tangling their relationship. Hank wants the kind of life he had with his ex-wife. Larry wants to have his sexual freedom without apologizing or lying about it. He is astonished at seeing two gay men in a kind of marriage. It hits him hard when he recognizes that the two men who most seem heterosexual—like the "normal" men he has grown up among and tried to be and believes he is not— are the ones who are most in love.

Love. It is more important than sex. Though his appetite for the sex he has never experienced with any other human being on the planet is ravenous each and every day, he wants love more. Emotions impossible to voice swirl within him as he hears one man directly declare his love for another man. And knowing they love despite the problems in their marriage of a sort, they pledge to try and make it work. Because that is how much they love.

It is nearly incomprehensible to him. It doesn't match anything he has ever read or ever heard about homosexual men. But now the possibility has been made flesh, and this possibility is a kind of miracle: *Love between gay men exists.*

In his final scene after the game is concluded, Harold aims his piercing monologue at Michael. Harold's assertion that Michael is "a homosexual and you don't want to be, but there's nothing you can do to change it…you'll always be a homosexual…Always. Until the day you die," read as if a sentence was being handed down by a pitiless judge. But in this moment of their performance, his words seem brutal only in their inescapable truth.

For Harold is merely speaking fact. Hard, unbreakable fact Michael has been running from all his life. But the kicker of it all is his last line to Michael. "Call you tomorrow."

As Donald holds the broken, sobbing Michael after everyone has departed, a new perception emerges that perhaps friendship is as important as love. Friendship. Understanding. Compassion. This is what Donald offers Michael, and he is seized with want for the same—to say everything he has held back for his entire life, to wail out all his anguish, and simply be accepted as he does so.

And not with his phantom friend created from a ten-second passing, but with someone flesh and blood in the present moment.

The screen is completely dark for a second as Michael shuts the door behind him on his way to a midnight Mass. From his peripheral vision he sees many of the men in the audience leap out of their seats, scurrying their way up the aisles, their heads down. But he stays through the closing credits. Another habit learned from his father. Besides, he does not want to yet break the spell. Each character is shown one at a time with the name of the actor portraying them. He restrains himself from applauding as if he is at a live performance. But he wishes he could give a standing ovation and yell "Bravo!" for every last one.

An unconscious exhale escapes him as the screen goes to black. The loop of inert commercials returns. He puts on his brown suede bomber jacket, a gift from Christmas that pleased him immeasurably. It had provided his parents much pleasure in giving it, as well as relief, for it had been too long since they had seen him smile that openly, his guard down.

He exits his row, determined to hold his head up while leaving. Everyone else is gone. Or so he thinks until he spots someone slumped over in his seat in the second to the last row of the center section. As soon as he notices this person, they raise their head at that exact same moment, meeting his face. The person removes his round wire rim glasses, wipes his eyes (*has the guy been crying?*), and says with a timid, weak smile, "I'm sorry."

He is so taken aback by this mystifying apology he can only manage a sputtering "Wh...what?"

The guy puts the wire rim glasses back on, stands up, smooths his heavy sweater, and shyly declares again, "I'm sorry."

This time he can only think to say, "It's OK."

The guy mutters, "It's all so sad," as he walks, but doesn't rush, out of the row. They glance at each other. The guy is, if not his own age, then only older by a couple of years. Same height, but thinner. It's hard to tell the color of his eyes which appear quite large and round behind the glasses. His hair is light blond and abundant, but conservatively cut on the sides and at the back of his neck. They silently walk into and through the theater lobby. Not side-by-side, but not at a distance either.

The sky is grayer, and the cold is heavier than when he came in two-and-a-half hours earlier. He starts to head up the street in the direction of the library, unsure what to say. The guy falls into step walking with him, saying nothing.

Where the guy is going, he has no idea. But he's glad they are together even as he feels nervous and awkward.

They walk about seven blocks in silence. Then, out of nowhere, the guy gently murmurs, "If we could just learn not to hate ourselves quite so very much," repeating a line Michael says during his after-party breakdown. The guy adds no words of his own.

They walk on in silence, getting nearer the library.

But he cannot, will not, let those words hang there between them as if he is in agreement. "What Michael says is true. For *him*. But even Donald says that Michael is better now than what he's been in the past. And I don't think Hank and Larry hate themselves at all. The cowboy doesn't hate himself. And Donald and Harold may not always like themselves, but they don't hate themselves the way Michael does. Emory and Bernard too. Maybe they're unhappy at times and regret playing the telephone game, but they have good things too. Work, sex, friends. They don't hate themselves."

More walking. More silence.

And then the guy asks in a whisper so soft it's as if he's afraid the question will be heard, "What about you?"

He feels a stabbing pain in his heart. But he won't show it. He makes a conscious effort not to stop or walk faster. Or let his voice betray his feelings. "Sometimes," he says, after a moment.

Walking. Silence.

"But I'm going to live in New York City. And I'm going to write plays. I'm going to be on Broadway. I'm going to find a lover. And I'm going to have lots of friends. So many friends. All who are…ga…gay," he stammers. "Homosexual. Whatever you want to call them. No. Call *us*." The dam has busted. He smiles, then blathers on enthusiastically, almost giddy. "And we're all going to fantastic parties and get drunk and smoke pot and dance and laugh and cry and play truth games that are so extremely honest we can never ever lie to ourselves or each other about anything ever again. And we'll comfort one another and hold each other tight. And we'll always get through to the next day no matter what."

The other guy stops, inhales. When he lets out his breath, he speaks bashfully but with indisputable delight. "Well, that sounds pretty good to me." He turns and offers a smile along with his extended hand. "I'm Mark."

"My name's Robby," he replies.

◆◆◆

Two days later, he gets a 'C-' on the calculus test, its own miracle given he never opened the textbook the rest of the weekend. The following Saturday, he meets Mark at Kentucky Wesleyan College. It turns out he is an engineering major in his sophomore year. After a tour of the campus and lunch at Jerry's Diner, the popular student burger joint nearby, they spend the afternoon in Mark's dorm room. They talk and talk and talk. They listen to Janis Joplin's just released *Pearl* album and *After the Gold Rush* by Neil Young, then move to Cat Steven's *Tea for the Tillerman*. At some point, after switching to *Sly and the Family Stone's Greatest Hits*, their fingers touch, they kiss, they are naked, and Robby experiences his first orgasm from a blow job with an electrical intensity he did not know his body contained.

They are secret boyfriends until May, when Mark returns home to *his* small Southern town in Virginia. Mark never comes back, writing him in early August that he is engaged to his longtime high school girlfriend and says this is his last letter. Despite the stream of letters Robby mails afterward, Mark stays true to his word.

Robby graduates a year later and goes to the University of Kentucky in the fall of 1972 for longer than he plans. Eventually, he makes his way to New York City where he is Robert instead of Robby. He becomes part of an off-off-Broadway theatre company that puts on six of his plays. Four are published as actor's editions by Samuel French, Inc. and the Dramatists Play Service. None of his work is ever produced on a Broadway stage.

More importantly than the difference between sex and love, he also learns the difference between romance and love. At one point he meets a director where all three ebb and flow, occasionally coming into perfect balance. He and the director stay together for many, many years.

And whenever anyone asks him what his all-time favorite movie is, he always answers *The Boys in the Band*.

# Ideal Lover Wanted

Seeking a sexy nekkid angel who pays his bills.

Should be named Kevin or Shane. Blonde. Blue-eyed (or green). Superb surfer's body or a gymnast, farm boy, skateboard punk's build. Intact, handsomely proportioned, thick but not particularly large penis with low-hanging, smooth-to-the-touch shaved balls, all surrounded by a thickly matted field of golden blonde pubic hair one can graze in. Same-colored hair, but more lightly spread, across his firm, flat chest, and taut tan nipples.

Plays the saxophone, sews, or collects quilts. Is learning carpentry so he can make his own rocking chair. Can handle all the treachery of modern technology. Will teach or learn with me the patience of gardening. Would like to raise a pet—well, a dog, never a cat—from infancy. No children.

Knows enough of the woods to spend at least a weekend hiking and camping, sleeping outside with the stars—happy, unafraid, and uncomplaining. But has no objections to the indulgences of luxury and extravagance at a fine hotel on occasion. First priority for travel in the United States is New Orleans; overseas, Greece.

Will dawdle away rainy afternoons at art galleries or in front of the television watching old black-and-white movies or classics from the 1960s and 1970s. In fact, likes television but knows when to turn it off and *never* has it on just for background noise. Has an eclectic taste in music that dismisses nothing. Insatiably reads a lot of everything, but more fiction and poetry than nonfiction.

Loves to eat and occasionally feast. Favorites cuisines are Mexican, Italian, French, Chinese, Thai, Indian, and Ethiopian. Is not an alcoholic or in recovery and can hold his liquor, enjoys beer, wine, champagne, Bloody Marys, dry vodka martinis with olives, margaritas, and all the rest. Smokes or ingests a little pot occasionally. Takes no other drugs. Will make himself exercise and sweat and do the work to stay in shape and unaddicted. Pushes me (with affection) to do the same.

Has a great sense of humor from silly-ridiculous slapstick to coldly cynical Wildean wit. Knows the black comedy of life but believes in karma, consciousness, kindness, or at least has some mystical bent without being dogmatic. Enjoys silence, especially that of nature, but doesn't need prompting to dance his ass off to blaring wild music.

Is totally, indiscriminately, out of the closet. Active in some volunteer, public service way.

An aura of health, holiness, and happiness radiates from him.

Knows that sometimes we both just need to be apart and alone, and it doesn't mean anything more than we just need to be apart and alone.

In sex, no restrictions. Well, perhaps one or two easily negotiated. No roles to play, and all roles to play. Romantic, experimental, sensual, ritualistic, tender, loud, unabashed sex as we feel and know the moment for hours on end. Lusts to make eye contact while fucking and when coming.

All of this would be nice but is not necessary.

# The Last Great Aria of a Magnificent Faggot

He seems more fantastical creature than human being. Face powdered chalk white, cheeks brilliantly rouged, eyes shadowed royal purple with a tiny line of glittering gold in the uppermost lid, and the lashes expanded by mascara deep black and spidery. His luxuriantly thick silver-and-blue-tinted hair is immaculately coiffed in an upward sweep. He wears a spectacular gold caftan with emerald green and ruby red threading in hieroglyphic patterns woven throughout, accessorized with a long champagne silk scarf knotted loosely around the folds of his ancient turkey-creased neck. The caftan envelops his emaciated frame; the scarf hangs all the way down to his skeletal waist.

What I find so fascinating in all this is the detail that is missing—nothing has been applied to his pinkish, wrinkled lips. No bold colored lipstick, no pop of liner tracing their wide, thin journey around his mouth, no moisturizing lotions to soften their prune-like dryness. Nothing to intensify their appearance or smooth and lessen their age. The pale, flaked, disappearing lips are his only concession to being ninety-six years old.

He is commandingly clear that he is not a drag queen, and this is not a drag outfit. "It is simply what I choose to wear at this time of my life," he declares in the wavering watery voice of an ancient man. "It is what is most *comfortable* and what is most true for me to wear *now*," he emphasizes.

"Why do you call yourself a 'faggot'?" I ask.

"I don't call myself anything," he answers. "I *name* myself. The first great wisdom everyone should know, and everyone would be much happier in abiding: *Name oneself.* In naming myself, I *claim* myself. And, in my specificity of self, I am many things, many personae, many people, within my ninety-six years. Hell! Within my last ninety-six minutes. My last ninety-six *seconds*! And within all of it, I am most essentially a faggot. It is the only word that approaches anywhere near to encapsulating all that I am. And please note I don't name myself A Faggot. I name myself, A *Magnificent* Faggot."

He states this last sentence piercing me with striking, still luminous eyes with flecks of startling green. It is a frank, appraising gaze almost daring me to disagree with him, but there's a conspiratorial glint of delight as well. As if I'm being challenged (or invited?) to be as frank and daring in return. He then punctuates his expression with a barely discernible smile of such bemused mystery I am reminded of a withered but no less captivating Mona Lisa. I bite my tongue lightly, so I won't break out in laughter at my surprise of being charmed by this ninety-six-year-old antique of an era long gone.

"Most people find 'faggot' an offensive and hateful word, the queer equivalent of the n-word," I say, coaxing him on for further explanation of his fierce commitment to this naming.

"First and foremost," he sighs impatiently, "you keep forgetting what I have so well-established, and which should by now be so prominently obvious since you first approached me for this rare interview for which you should be grateful I am granting. I am not now, nor have I ever been, nor will I ever be, that truly most offensive and hateful moo-cow term of them all, 'most people.'"

"But the community..."

"The second most offensive moo-cow term. 'The community!' I am always and absolutely a community of one."

This irritates me. "Do you feel no responsibility to the rest of us?"

"My only allegiance is to my art." He is the one irritated now.

"But the queer community—"

"How hideously hypocritical you are! To imply criticism of me for naming myself as 'faggot' while you so easily pass 'queer' through your lips and believe it appropriate to denigrate the thousands of us still alive who know acutely its cutting scars in decades past."

"We reclaimed the word—"

"We? *I* was not consulted about this reclamation of the term 'queer.'" There is no trace of an old man's wavery pitch now. Instead, an angry, unexpectedly tough timbre holds his words.

I nervously reposition the angle of my phone currently recording this conversation. It sits atop a glass table between us, bearing his two-olive vodka martini in its long-stemmed, wide-brimmed clear glass.

He won't let me film him. He says that if he is to be filmed, then I must truly utilize the medium of cinematography. That means composed imagery and the intelligent arrangement of key lighting photographed on film stock no longer used in this "degraded visual age of boring, bland digits and pixels or whatever they are" of video recording. At first, I wondered if he was simply vain in his refusal to be shown as old as he is. But I've come to recognize that this is yet another odd principle by which he is determined to live until the end, even if it is rooted in an aesthetic of the vanished past. He was *meant* for the big screen, and that meant to be *on* film in the shadowy shades of silver created by black-and-white cinematography, or else in the vibrant candy box Technicolor of 1940s musicals. There is simply no valid substitute that could be made.

I decide to back down a notch. Subduing any aggressive tone, I ask in a friendly, conversational one, "But isn't 'queer' the most inclusive term to describe all of us in the LGBTQIA2S+ alphabet?"

He will not be swayed. "It does not describe *me* at all! Some queer 'community' holds no right to dictate how I name myself. And if it tries to do so, it is not a 'community.' It is a cult!"

"But homophobic people use 'faggot' as a weapon of hate and violence," I push back.

"As they did with 'queer.'"

"Which is why we reclaimed it!"

His eyes narrow in silent threat, then he turns away from me briefly. When he faces me again, he talks with unhurried, calm steel. "I have no need to 'reclaim' the name 'faggot' because I never ceded my claim to it. To anyone. Ever. I am ninety-six years old. The door marked 'Exit' enlarges evermore, and behind it is a black hole swallowing this space called 'my life.' I will not spend what remains of my life, be it ten more minutes or ten more years, discussing things that bore me. I will not discuss something, much less *defend* something, that is an unchangeable fact: everyone is free to name oneself; indeed, it is their responsibility at some point to do so. I take that away from no one, and no one will ever take that away from me. I name myself A Magnificent Faggot and there is no further discussion to be had."

But my steel remains as well. "We can return to this question of how you identify yourself later."

He rises from the plush cardinal red throne he has been sitting. He roars, "We will not return to it ever. Ask a question about another subject or leave. Choose *now*!"

I suck in my breath, shocked at how much anger this outrageous, flamboyant gay scarecrow has within him. I know I can't let him control our interview, but I also have no doubt he will prevent me from going any further if I do not relent immediately.

I consider that maybe he has a right to name himself A Magnificent Faggot after all, as wrong and offensive as the word is. Having survived so much queer history for so many tumultuous decades, perhaps he has earned it. His cult reputation as a writer began with one scandalous volume of extravagantly romantic, religiously-infused erotic poetry celebrating every male homosexual act ever imagined, detailed in explicit, florid verse. Published in the 1950s, it was the center of a minor censorship struggle that saw him jailed for nearly three months on pornography charges before the conviction was overturned.

He also wrote two controversial underground novels in the 1960s. *Night is Where the Truth Lies*, appearing at the height of the civil rights movement, is the story of an interracial gay male couple's long-term relationship and the plantation slave scenarios they enact. His second novel, *Ours Alone*, describes four encounters of father-son incest—the first when the son is only sixteen with the final one occurring thirty-five years later, months before the father's death.

With such dues paid, maybe there is no need to keep trying to change his mind over his use of the word "faggot."

Somehow, readers periodically rediscover his poems or novels. Some even become ardent acolytes. They are famished to read anything and everything they can find written by or about him. Original editions of his books are highly prized by this miniscule but fervent following. Readers are known to have paid in the low hundreds for unauthorized, smeary-inked, poorly bound bootleg reprints that flourished in the late 1990s when his writings were long out of print and nearly impossible to find.

Minor as he is, an academic literary journal article will sporadically note him in an aside or footnote. And one published a lengthy critical assessment of his writing in the late nineties during the bootleg mania. My hope is to publish a profile on this essentially forgotten figure for a print magazine like *The New Yorker* that will lead to a book contract. His work needs to be analyzed through a twenty-first-century queer lens, no doubt. But the time is also ripe for him to be noted as an unsung transgressive queer male writer of the previous century— a more queeney and radical outlier than Burroughs or Ginsberg, a cohort he steadfastly refuses to ever associate himself, considering them inferior literary talents.

He knows all this and is willing to play along with me for now. My intuition is that, besides his curiosity regarding my project and the potential it holds for his work reprinted in new editions, he finds me a curious, even pleasant, distraction. Although the idea of any sexual activity with him repulses me, rumors are whispered of young men in their late teens and twenties finding their way to his apartment. His stories and poems are revelations to them, transforming their understanding of the universe itself and their place in it. He is a visionary of the sexual and the spiritual they must be near. It is said they kneel before him to suck his cock or stand stripped of their clothes to masturbate in front of him, ejaculating upon his naked chest, which he considers "a holy anointment."

I choose to surrender. For now. Soothingly, I say, "So, please tell me about your work."

And with that, he smiles his Mona Lisa smile, bows to me with slow graciousness, and seats himself once again with great, gentle dignity. "Yes. That is the reason why we are doing this after all." He is genuinely hospitable, ready to take me into his confidence, or at least pretend that he is. It's as if the arrowed antagonism of the previous moment never occurred.

"What would you say is the key theme explored in all of your writing?" I query, professionally engaged and polite.

"I am an artist. I am always the key theme my work explores. As is true for most artists, I am my own fetish."

"So, your novels and poems are in some ways autobiographical?"

"That is the obvious question the unsubtle minded most often ask."

It is hopeless to decipher what his game is here. Within the space of two sentences, he has cheerfully provided me with a quotable bon mot and then slyly insulted me. But I persist, and I suspect that is what he most wants from me. "The question may be obvious, but it is fair. If you are, as you say, always the key theme of your work, then it's reasonable to ask if the stories you write are based on your actual life."

"It is reasonable. And reasonableness is antithetical to art...at least to *faggot* art."

His smile is falsely placid, but the green-flecked eyes are dancing with devilish mischief. He obviously enjoys taunting and goading me, but I am more confident than ever that this is a form of play (or foreplay?) for him. He wants me to respond in some way he can happily deem worthy of his intellect and spirit.

"Then, why don't you explain it all for me like Sister Mary Ignatius does in Christopher Durang's satire of Catholic education," I lob across the net. But then I correct myself. "Catholic *indoctrination*, I mean."

He lights up. "Bravo! Brava! And I'll even throw in a nonbinary 'Bravx!' You *are* a quick learner. And bravo, brava, bravx for not adding a 'please.' I didn't deserve it."

But I don't want him to engineer an opportunity to digress, so I set aside this compliment which could also be potential bait. "You were saying the theme of your art is always yourself."

His eyes spark happily again, and he smiles broadly without artifice. He takes a pause and considers before speaking. "Yes. Whether the story is true-life experience merely reported or is partial experience reshaped, or a complete and absolute spinning of made-up make-believe is the least interesting, least crucial, aspect of it. No matter the origins of the story, what is more revealed, what is most elemental, what is most determinative to its telling is my imagination and my empathy. How far I go, how profound I bore into this compassionate projection...in this, I am forever exposed, forever the subject, forever the theme. Empathetic imagination is the vital blood of all my writing as it is of all art. Ultimately, it is our only saving grace as human beings."

Even though there is an element of performance here, he means every word he is saying. It's the most he has yet to reveal of himself. In my excitement at having reeled him in to this degree, I impatiently jump to the most important aspect I want to interrogate. "You are aware, of course, that there are those who say your imagination and empathy are...*extreme*. Dangerous. Even damaging."

His long, veiny arm reaches out for the martini glass that has been untouched for a while. He sips the last of it, sits the glass back down, and appraises me with unnerving, expressionless detachment. His eyes locked on me, I feel like I am some sort of prey ready to be captured and clawed.

I hate that I can't lock my eyes on his and remain equally steady and willful. Hot and flushed, I avert my face from his and glance around the confining room. It's difficult to discern what color the walls are painted, in part due to the low yellow cast of the stained-glass lamp on the end table, but primarily because of the numerous paintings, drawings, photographs, prints, and movie posters hanging on them. The artwork, including sculptures standing in various places, is from every historical period and school. More than a few are of male nudes. There are even photographs and cartoons cut out from magazines and newspapers scotch-taped to the walls, covering whatever gaps may have existed.

What is not covered by the artwork is blocked by seemingly endless shelves of books. They are a chaotic jumble where Euripides, Shakespeare, Tolstoy, Chekov, and Joyce promiscuously intermingle with Jaqueline Susann, Stephen King, Edna Ferber, Irving Wallace, and Dan Brown.

I look down and note the mismatched rugs of assorted colors, patterns, fabrics, and sizes. What looks like a cheap ghastly pink bathroom rug is the crossing "T" to a long narrow exquisite piece of Persian carpet. Glancing back up, I take in the dazzling arrays of fresh spring flowers—brilliant red roses, large white lilies, purple mignon dahlias, orange hibiscuses. They are arranged in a gamut of vases varying from cheap plastic to intricate jade marvels. I wonder who sends or brings all these floral treasures to his fourth-floor walk-up in the transitioning Polk Street neighborhood bordering the Tenderloin.

Even though I have not been looking at him, I am positive he has been following me as I have surveyed the walls, the floor, the flowers.

At last, he speaks. Amazingly, his voice is quite soft, even tender. "I don't give a good goddamn what other people say about me or my writing. But in this present now, I do give a good goddamn what *you* say about it."

I'm somewhat astonished by his invitation. It is reasonable that he would want to engage my thoughts on his work, but I assumed such a conversation would come much later in the process. It is hard to fathom: Are we already in such a space where he cares what I think about his writing? Or is this a form of flirtation? Or a trap of some kind? Inexplicably, I feel exposed.

"Surely, you have an opinion," he prods softly.

"It's certainly easy to see why your writing...especially your two novels were..." I begin.

"*Were*?" he questions in mock umbrage.

"*Are*," I quickly amend. We exchange silly smiles, and he even exhales a mild chuckle. Is it possible that he's as nervous as I am? "Your novels are compelling to read. They're transgressive without any apology. Often, though, it's apparent why others find your work...wrong," I risk, then gulp. But there is no reaction or change in his demeanor, so I press on. "You put me so inside your character's skins, their consciousness. To such a degree I feel like I'm living their lives and thinking their thoughts. Intently...feeling these people as I read them," I rush out. "But...but...well, it is hard to put into words."

"It is always hard to put into words. But putting it into words is the whole point."

"Well...the violence. It not only is disturbing, it also feels disturbed." The sharp, quick intake of his breath throws me. But I know if I stop now and make any attempt to backpedal, he will be even more severe. "In *Night is Where the Truth Lies* you have the interracial couple acting out plantation master and slave roles complete with iron shackles, heavy chains, and brutal whippings. The white character is always the master, and the Black character is always the slave."

"They're dedicated to historical accuracy," he deadpans.

"That's a horrible thing to joke about!" I am indignant. "The way you portray these issues of race and violence and sexuality are exceptionally problematic. Some would even say traumatic."

"So, the transgressive has now become the traumatic."

"I understand that you aspired to resolve the Black character's inner conflict of racial self-hatred imposed upon him by a racist white dominant society..." I'm grappling, reaching too hard to explain.

"*'Aspired'*? Meaning I did not achieve?"

A sudden resolve rises within me, and I am burning with certainty: He *needs* to be told how his work is now seen by a new queer generation. And I am the one to do so. "Whatever you achieved or meant to achieve, you still reinforced the centuries-old systemic hierarchy of violent white domination over Black men. The interracial couple of your book maintain the cultural paradigms of white patriarchal oppression through sexualized violence."

He imperiously enunciates each word of his response as if I am the most stupid of children. "The interracial couple who are the basis for *Night is Where the Truth Lies* were the most loving, considerate, long-lasting couple, male or female, I have ever known. We were all good friends for many years until the white one, a professor of theater, withdrew from living in grievous self-pity when the Black one died. The Black partner was not an acclaimed, well-known, and widely loved actor and activist as in the novel. Making him a closet case famous star was the most fictional element of the book!"

"They told me all about their slave playing only two or three hours after we met. Mutual nakedness among strangers can make such revelations unfold with ease." He looks at me derisively before he scornfully adds, "But I doubt you would know anything about that. My assumption is that you prefer to read and theorize about sex and sexuality rather than experience it. They had whole lives of work, family, world travel, and yes, even church. They didn't act out plantation scenes every time they had sex. They weren't driven to do it as compulsion. They did it when they *wanted* to. When it was right for *them* to do it. They did not give a good goddamn about the 'paradigms' of 'oppression' of their sexual slave role-play. They never gave it a second's thought. Your mewling analysis and prissy judgments were *irrelevant* to them!"

He utters this last remark with vicious, curt dismissal. Despite his attempt at shaming me, I feel more resolute than ever. Like most, if not all, old gay white men, he is incapable of grasping the bigger political, social, and cultural contextualization. I shoot back, "Their dynamic becomes a pathway for unquestioned acceptance. Just like the father and son in *Ours Alone*. Without realizing it, you end up endorsing it. As if it is all just natural occurrence."

Leaning over as far as he can, coming right up into my face, his unyielding visage looks as if it has been chiseled out of granite. "I *always* realize what I am creating. And in the sense that in nature, in *human* nature, one finds sons and fathers having sex and interracial couples involved in erotic master and slave roles, such things *are* natural. And while there is much in nature of which I do not approve, I must accept. Because it is in nature. Because it is already there, it already exists. And I cannot change what is already there, what already exists. I can only utilize all my being to investigate and percieve it. All my mind and heart and soul. All my best, most courageous, and humane self must be brought to bear not only to understand and accept but, yes, to embrace and love these human natures."

These are the old familiar justifications for art and its disengagement with injustice that I will not sanction. "But the son is like the Black character in your other novel. He is never angry about it! Neither character is even traumatized by it. No one even regrets any of it. That's wrong!" I can hear a high, pinching whine creep into my voice.

"You are far more upset that the characters are not suffering burdens and punishments than by their actual experiences."

"Because they never become aware of how they are victims or oppressors. Much less question how they are manipulated or exploited into these roles by systemic institutionalized racism or patriarchal empowerment of toxic masculinity."

He shakes his head in severe disappointment. "You are young, and you hold firmly, noxiously, to beliefs others have inculcated within you. Beliefs that were no doubt presented as some great factual truth or brilliant intellectual sociopolitical analysis. But they are nothing more than fancifully spun crap. Theories and explanations—*illusions*, really—to navigate the mysteries that exist within the real lives of indefinable, messy, contradictory, ultimately unknowable human beings with their eternally mutating desires and fears and, most mysterious of all, their *choices* and paths of journey that are so vastly different from yours. As your life goes forward, stringent experience will teach you all you do not yet know, all that you cannot yet see. You whimper how wrong it is to portray a father and son in sex as if you know something of the world. *When you know nothing!* When I was thirteen back in the hills of Kentucky, my Papa caught me and a friend jacking off in the barn that summer, and he whipped me buck naked with all his might, using tree switches and rope and then his belt. Whipping me from the top of my head down to the soles of my feet and everywhere, *everywhere*, in between. And when he was done, he pulled me down with his fingers tangled in my hair, twisting it as tight and as painful as he knew how to hurt me, and he forced his dick into my mouth until he came."

I gasp, and tears sting my eyes. I stare at him, paralyzed, unable to form words.

He shakes his head again, pitying me. "How easy it is for you to believe *that*! However horrible it may be, you can still accept a father beating and raping his son as a fact that happens in this world. But the idea, the mere *consideration* within a novel—a work of art, or at least an attempt towards a work of art— that somewhere on this mad, insane planet a father and son could experience something loving and sexual between them, *intimacy* really...and I emphasize 'intimacy' because that is what truly disturbs you, an intimacy which confuses them and shakes them and alters them, but which they know expresses something there is no language for, that even *one* such father and son could exist and not be 'traumatized' or 'oppressed' by four such experiences over nearly forty years, is totally beyond your imagining. And acknowledging the possibility of that existence and writing about it to comprehend it with utmost identification and empathy, to give it its due, is *not* an endorsement of, or proselytizing for, incest of any kind. A qualifier, which in an educated, civilized society, would never even have need to be made—it is such an obvious given—

but now must be underlined and highlighted and stated in large capital letters for the weak and the literal-minded of this debased era."

I refuse to have any of this. "But the world cannot change unless art confronts and opposes the structural hierarchies of systemic, institutionalized power and oppression."

And with that, he raises himself out of the chair once more. From some source far within himself, he conjures a rumbling baritone. *"Enough!"* he shouts. "That is not art! That is *social work*!" he spits with blistering loathing. Changing the world is the vocation for those who dare not change themselves. In large part because they do not know themselves. That is why they fear art! Because they are too timid, too terrified, to confront, much less change, who *they* are. So, of course, they must change the world. Such a puny thing. Such a...*missionary* thing to do! Create art! Create love! Have the courage to dedicate your life to those and only those. *Then* you will experience such oppression and terrors from the 'structural hierarchies of systemic, institutionalized power,' you may never survive."

Some sort of mystical transfiguration is taking place. He is standing erect, proud, noble. The full splendor of his regalia takes in the room's light and reflects it back in riotous peacock colors. His bearing is charismatic, his voice supremely magisterial. Decades have fallen away from his being, and for a brief span of minutes, he is his most potent, unstoppable, unquenchable younger self, returned to his peak.

"Look at yourself: If you would hear of the interracial couple of my first novel dissolving their relationship in rancor and bitterness and hate, or even in sadness and despair, over their tragic inability to enter the other's life in history, their failure to overcome all that racism has done to twist and shatter and defeat their love, you would then accept—hell, you would happily advocate and defend without any hesitation or wonderment—*that* outcome as the believable, right and 'natural' resolution for who they are and what they have done. But for you to hear of a twenty-plus year loving interracial male couple converting their heritages and histories into something primal and erotic that is also healing, that *defeats* their heritages and histories, *that* is beyond your grasp of imagination. Don't you see? *You* are the one who denies them their full humanity! You are the one who most oppresses them! You are the one who most voraciously demands they reinforce 'paradigms of institutionalized racism and patriarchal toxic masculinity.' You refuse to see what is present that does not fit the patterns cut into your closed-off mind and walled-off heart. You costume and bejewel and perfume your political and cultural analysis with all sorts of dull, obfuscating, constipated jargon—the jargon of the academic. The activist. The *critic*. Those who would never dare risk the ridicule and condemnation they so profligately pour onto others, those others who may be geniuses or the rankest of amateurs, but who at least thrust forward to create. No. All you do with your stunted language and feeble theorizing is to regenerate the human race's original stupidity. You *reduce*! I know that the old world of the faggot, the old world of art, of beauty, of the romantic run wild and ravishing, that faggot world is rushing to its final fading, soon to be extinguished. And in its place will be those who hate the luxuriance of beauty, who hate the astonishment and uncontrolled ecstasy of art. Who wish always and only to reduce it all to the nauseous, vile mush of the tame and the puny and the pleasant. All of it, of course, buried under slabs and slabs of ruthless, meaningless, convoluted verbiage pretending to be radical dissection or, God help us, 'deconstruction,' in the service of—not of morality, for that would demand too much complexity, too much effort of subtlety and nuance and distinction of thought—no, not in the service of morality, but in the service of *moralism*. Easy, digestible spoonfuls of moralistic pablum making us all good little boys and girls, right-thinking and well-behaved, in this big, unjust, unfair world. A world that not only refuses to conform, but is intolerably indifferent, to all you want but cannot change about human nature and the living soul of it in art."

He is in a trance, eyes mercilessly penetrating mysteries only he can see. "Know this as irrevocable, eternal fact. *That* most assuredly will never be me! I cannot, I will not, ever be reduced. I will always embody art. I will always embody love. And barring love, then sex! Magnificent, raw, feral, unapologetic, shameless, nothing held back, all-annihilating sex! These are the only truths, the only religions. All else is distraction and rubbish. Worthless, wasteful, stupid shit. Sumptuous art! Undying, all-sacrificing, ecstatic love! Ecstatic sex! Opulent beauty! These are the only gods to worship, to create a life for! To *give* one's life to. To sacrifice...to *burn* one's life in service of. A Magnificent Faggot is the one who reduces nothing but creates all! A Magnificent Faggot is the *God* who creates himself! It is the most celestial, poetic name in the universe! *I PROCLAIM IT! I AM A MAGNIFICENT FAGGOT!*"

He stands exultant. Justified. *Completed*. His face is soaked in perspiration, causing the powder and rouge to run in long melting lines. His tear-glinted eyes are affixed somewhere far away, taking in a thunderous ovation of adoring acclaim only he can hear. His smile is rapturous.

And suddenly, as if unplugged from the powerful source of energy that has fueled him during his long operatic exclamation, he collapses in exhaustion, bereft and empty of all sustenance. He is now unquestionably a stooped, quavering nonagenarian. His eyes are wide and unseeing as he scours the room. Slashed with fear, he seem not to know who he is or where he is at.

Alarmed and frightened, I rush to him. "Are you alright? Should I call an ambulance?"

"No, no," he responds feebly.

His ghostly streaked face with its bewildered stare distresses me. His breathing is slow and strained. A death rattle? "Are you sure you don't need an ambulance?" I ask again.

"No." Then, remembering his manners, "Thank you." Something weaves into his consciousness, and he falteringly finds a way to his throne.

"What can I do for you?" I plead.

"Brandy. There." He points to a low metal cart with three levels of trays. It looks cheap and homemade, but the flawless cut crystal decanter sitting atop most certainly is not. "Pour two snifters. We will make a toast to my last great aria." He is trying to rouse himself to his previous outré flair.

"Are you sure you don't need a doctor?"

"It is always inspiring to see such kindness in one so young," he says meekly. "But, no, thank you. What I most need is something warm and carnal on my tongue. That is all that is required. And then perhaps some poetry. And a prayer. And then sleep." His words come out protracted and labored.

"I think I should call a doctor."

"Do *not* call a doctor. *Do* go pour two snifters of brandy, or at least pour one for *me*," he directs, his fire reigniting.

I do as instructed. When I return with his drink in hand, I kneel at the side of his throne and hand it to him, so he does not have to make the effort to reach up.

He smiles at me with sweet grandfatherly gentleness. "You have been good to me today," he says with quiet sincerity. "Indulgent. Thank you."

"No," I reply. "Thank you."

He holds up his brandy. "To you!" he proclaims. "For inspiring...well, perhaps *provoking* is more accurate," he notes, flashing an almost childlike smile, "...still, thank you with fondest gratitude for...*creating*...the conditions that inspired my final aria."

"You said 'last' before and now you call it 'final.'"

Savoring each deliberate sip, the brandy is restoring him. "Yes. Final. Death calls. It no longer whispers. Instead, it is an insistent, urgent foghorn guiding me towards it. The fastidiously cultivated, oh-so-lovingly-tended, marvelous, precious ego garden of *me*, A Magnificent Faggot, will soon...poof!" he makes the magic act gesture of disappearance, "Which is how it should be." He pauses and drifts away momentarily before returning with self-aware laughter. "Which is how it *is*, whether it should be or not! Besides, I've always thought living to an even one hundred years rather gauche." Revitalized, he points to a bottom shelf on one of the bookcases. "The largest photograph album. Take it out."

Once more, I do as I am told.

"Open it," he orders.

And so, I do. There are heavy pages of old black-and-white pictures, some glossy and slick, while others have been developed on an almost cardboard stock. They are of a young man who can't possibly be older than twenty-one or twenty-two, if that much. He is naked except for a g-stringed pouch covering his genitals. His hair is a wild dark forest, almost unnaturally thick and curly. His eyes are wide with a jubilant expression. He is very skinny but sinewy, his muscles and build obviously shaped from hard manual work rather than working out. The stomach has an almost imperceptible, barely present roundness lower down. As I flip through the pages, he is posed in a series of "serious" shots imitating classical Greek art. He is sometimes adorned with a laurel, holding a lute or warrior's spear, and is dressed in sandals with thin straps running up his calves.

"Is this physique porn from the 1960s?" I wonder aloud.

He lets loose a peal of laughter. "You compliment me by suggesting that I could have looked so impossibly young in the 1960s as I was fast approaching my forties by then."

"These are of you?" I ask, incredulous. I squint my eyes and methodically and meticulously investigate the photos. My earnest study stimulates more laughter from him.

"Honestly, are you incapable of conjuring at least a modicum of pretense to suppress your shock that, yes, I was once that young? And, yes, once stunningly handsome with a young man's beautiful body."

"You were handsome." I catch myself. I look up at him and smile, nodding, "Of course, you still *are*."

He couldn't be happier. He raises his snifter. "Bravo! Well covered!"

I keep poring through the pictures. There are dozens. I come across a new set where he is now completely nude. I'm mesmerized by the copious amount of pubic hair surrounding his cock. It's as dense and dark and tangled as the hair on his head. He is well-endowed, not unnaturally or pornographically so, but his cock is long with notable girth; there is an overhang of skin at the tip as he is also uncircumcised. Naked, his expression is often one of shyness. But he also displays a wide, ridiculous, lopsided grin that reminds me of a Huck Finn rascal from a children's book. He makes goofy, embarrassed faces in many of the pictures that elicit a probably just as goofy smile of my own. He does jumping jacks in one set. In another, he points to his penis in mock surprise. There is a naughty, caught-kid glee and wide-eyed wonderment as he looks at his cock in different states of tumescence, stiffening, and hardness. Later photos show him lying outside in a tall field of grass, streaks and puddles of come on his belly and chest, satiated and content. And there is one—my favorite—where he stands fully naked and erect, spread-eagled, head slightly thrown back, and arms outstretched and raised high as if holding the sun. While the photograph is most likely posed rather than candid, the expression of transcendence on his face is no performance. He is euphoric, transported, in communion with something that can only be named as soul.

In some of the pictures, I see his back. It has five or six distinct raised scars crisscrossing it.

"May I ask when these photos were taken?"

"In 1940. Before I shipped off overseas." He speaks faintly, dreamily. "I lied about my age to enlist. I had just turned seventeen. And please don't be dull. I was not some naive child victim of dirty old men. In those days, one could be seventeen and very much a man moving about in the world with a man's responsibilities to family, which is one of the reasons I joined. One less mouth for my Papa and Mama to feed. And out of duty to my country, as perverted as that honorable ideal has been subsumed by faux patriotism and the parasitic corporate profiteers of war. It was a romantic time when young men knew life could end in a split-second, so all life was excitement and risk and adventure. I was a man, not a boy, at seventeen. And quite appreciated, respected, and often very well rewarded by the attention and praise and, yes, even friendship, of the artists and older queens of New York City's homosexual demimonde. Men knew how to be friends with each other then, including the older faggots and the young soldiers who were open to the cash or the company or the entree into refined society. It wasn't all sordid and tawdry and exploiting as so many would prefer to make it. Many of the queens, especially the artistic ones, were kind and generous, wanting to mentor and teach. I was a muse, and I was in God's great faggot heaven having my photograph taken in all manner of dress and undress."

There is something hypnotic about the pictures. I examine them keenly. I am absorbed by the expressions on his face. They radiate a quality, an element, I am unable to name. The word eludes me.

I look back to him. Our faces fix upon each other with affection. We hold our mutual gaze in silence for a while.

"I can see the you of then in the eyes of the you now. And I can see the you now in the eyes of the you then." My voice quivers. "It's almost...poetic."

The expression he gives to me is almost exactly the one he has in the photograph of him nakedly, exuberantly embracing the sky. There is so much acceptance—love, really—holding me in it. When he speaks, he is teasing and sheerly playful. "How wonderful," he says in an exaggerated deadpan. "You aren't *entirely* literal after all."

I don't know why, but I find this hilarious, and we both break out into raucous, boisterous laughter, our eyes dancing upon each other.

The word then comes to me. The word that most encapsulates his essence, the life force that has sustained him through the decades shared by the seventeen-year-old boy in the photographs and the ninety-six-year-old Magnificent Faggot in front of me now. That word is innocence.

# His Father

It is a Sunday evening nearly three months after Jonathan Lake's final session in Dr. Miriam Birnbaum's Tuesday Evening Therapy Group for Adult Male Survivors of Childhood and Adolescent Incest and Sexual Abuse. His father is napping, the Sunday newspaper he insists on reading in print form only spread across his chest. They are in Jonathan's miniscule condo with his father on the sand-toned living room sofa and Jonathan nearby in the kitchen with its louvered divider open, allowing him to peek out.

They had dinner tonight at the Porter Grill, a classic San Francisco steakhouse of the 1950s recently renovated to its former glory, having attended the musical version of *The Color Purple* earlier that afternoon. Father and son both laughingly admitted to thirsting for a proper martini as the appropriate means to transport themselves into the retro spirit of the restaurant. Still, neither was about to place hard-won—and in his father's case, long-standing—sobriety at such jeopardy. They remained alcohol-free, at least for another day.

When awake and active, his widower father was still handsome. Apart from a few fine lines around his brown eyes, his square face with its hard jaw was hardly blemished by time. He had a relatively trim build thanks to endless rounds of golf, his one and only mainstay of exercise. But sleep allowed his father's sixty-eight years to surface, exposing him as an undeniably old man. The face sagged, became heavier. A slight thickening of his middle has become more noticeable. Even his impeccably brushed short gray hair seemed flat and thin. Most concerning to Jonathan, however, was his father's unconscious breathing that wheezed as if strenuous effort was being made to keep air coming in and going out. He was not as strong or steady a man as he projected during his waking hours.

Jonathan knew his father's vulnerabilities more than he ever wanted to. His previous alcoholism was not an excuse for what he had done to Jonathan, but it was the primary factor explaining how their incest had come to pass. Having often retraced how it had all begun, Jonathan firmly believed that if his father had not been drunk that first time nothing would have ever happened between them. And with that door unopened, that line not crossed, there would never have been any other such occasions.

Inebriated and in a panic that he would urinate all over himself and the expensive rugs before he could reach the master bedroom, his father had barged into the bathroom shared by Jonathan and his sister without even a knock on the door. Fifteen-year-old Jonathan was standing naked in front of the mirror after a shower, erect, rehearsing faces and poses that might make him look sexually desirable. It all happened at such an incomprehensible speed that Jonathan froze, unable to reach his bath towel as his father furiously pissed into the toilet. From that moment on, everything else that ensued unfolded in an unreal slow motion that was equally incomprehensible to him. And remained so for a very long time, even after it had ended two years later.

His sleeping father stirs anxiously on the couch, his face contorting in an ugly grimace as if Jonathan's memory has been teleported into his dreams. He makes a barely audible whimper.

Seeing and hearing this, Jonathan is pierced with love for his father. He feels the deep urge to protect him. He is afraid such dreams might kill him. Jonathan is not ready—may never be ready, he admits—to say goodbye and let go of this man who enrages, moves, repulses, and inspires him in roiling, unequal measure. He thinks of the white-and-blue polka-dotted quilt his mother made for him before he went off to college—one of her most loving actions in her own dark drinking days—and considers bringing it from his bedroom to cover his father. But Jonathan is afraid that much movement and change of texture on his body might waken him.

It was during a family therapy session while Jonathan was in rehab for his own out-of-control alcoholism that the incest was at last confronted. He had privately decided he was never going to share that experience in any way as part of his individual or group therapy. When his father realized that Jonathan's time in treatment was soon coming to an end without his ever having admitted, much less examined, what had transpired for him as a teenager, he was the one to blurt out the truth. Through heaving, anguished sobs, he wailed, "Jonny is killing himself because I sexually abused him." The sixty-day stay in treatment was extended by thirty days more.

The therapist at the rehab center had a series of considered, disturbing conversations with Jonathan as to whether he wanted to report his father's incest to the police. Jonathan was clearheaded in his decision not to do so. Too much had changed—his father had now been sober for several years; his mother had died from cancer, leaving his father a widower; Jonathan's sister Sarah, who lived in Phoenix and rarely visited, had immediately forbidden her father to ever see his two young grandchildren again. His father in prison would not return Jonathan to sobriety or help his life find a way out of its current morass.

Jonathan trusted his father wholeheartedly when he swore to him and his sister that he had never touched, molested, or sexually acted out with any other teenager or child, male or female, before or after Jonathan. He had, in fact, never had an affair with anyone in his thirty-plus years marriage. Though he never revealed it to either his therapist or his father, Jonathan had made a drunken deep dive into both his father's desktop computer and laptop weeks before finally admitting he needed treatment. He found no history of dark web searches or downloads of sexually deviant pictures and videos, or even visits to websites of a mildly pornographic nature, heterosexual or homosexual.

His father stirs again in his sleep, wincing. He had complained earlier of shoulder and lower back pain exacerbated from "twisting too damn fast" while golfing. His usual quick steps had been more cautious this afternoon, and he had embarrassedly asked Jonathan if they could hail a taxi to the Porter Grill rather than continue walking. Jonathan was amused his father thought of taxis instead of Uber or Lyft. But he was also struck by how humbled, even ashamed, he seemed in making the request.

Jonathan and his father's routine is to see each other every couple of Sundays. They alternate between Jonathan taking the train to his father's newer, more manageable single-floor house in Mountain View and his father driving into San Francisco. They almost always go to a movie, then take a long walk through Golden Gate Park or along the Embarcadero when in San Francisco, and end up at a restaurant, some trendy and upscale, though they prefer small family-owned neighborhood places with a specific ethnic cuisine.

Their talk is usually easy and unstilted, but they rarely go into much personal territory beyond checking out the other's sobriety and any struggles that arise surrounding it. Even more rarely do they talk about anything of the past and nothing about the incest. Jonathan sometimes senses his father's tenuous attempts to do so, but he deflects him, afraid he will hear something new and unknown he will not be able to bear. Jonathan has borne enough of his father's unruly life, and the equanimity between them now suits him. He does not want anything more.

His father wakes suddenly, quite shaken. His eyes then droop briefly, and it seems as if he is fast asleep once more. But his head shoots up. Though still vaguely disoriented, he looks over to Jonathan and chuckles. "Part of getting old. I say I'm going to close my eyes for ten minutes and then I'm out cold for two hours."

"It hasn't been that long," Jonathan assures him. "Just a half-hour."

"Well, it will just make me stay awake that much later tonight," his father says. He yawns loud and long, but shudders horribly as he raises his arms. "Damn!" He quickly brings them down. "God, I hate getting old. It's always something hurting or not working." His father lifts himself agonizingly off the sofa accompanied by a not entirely exaggerated groan. He makes his way toward the bathroom a few feet away. "The other problem of getting old. You've always got to pee."

"Would you like me to make some coffee or tea?" Jonathan inquires.

"You know what I would really like?" his father asks, turning to face him. "I would love to have a cup of hot cocoa." He stops, amused at himself for a moment. "Isn't that odd? I haven't had hot cocoa or wanted hot cocoa in ages."

"That's not odd at all. Now that you've said it, I'd like to have some too. It's been a long time. Besides, it's a cold night."

His father makes his trip to the bathroom. The door is closed, but it is impossible for Jonathan not to hear him pissing. A strong, healthy stream, he notes.

Jonathan pulls out a saucepan from a lower cabinet and fills it with low-fat milk to warm. He then gathers sugar and vanilla to mix with the unsweetened cocoa powder. After stirring it all in, he opens an upper cabinet and takes down two ornate china cups and saucers. They are delineated with fine pinkish-red etchings of eighteenth-century English lords and ladies in grand finery, a sumptuous countryside manor in the background. His mother loved this tea set. His father was happy to give it to him when it was time to let go of their family home after her death.

His mother would sometimes make a delightful fuss serving hot chocolate in these cups to Jonathan and Sarah on cold or rainy days when they were small children. All of them would pretend they were at high tea with the most upper crust of English society. She would put on a broad, fake British accent and fancy airs that made Jonathan laugh out loud. It was so rare to see her silly and playful.

As Jonathan pours the steaming chocolate milk into a china teapot with matching etchings, he realizes how much more often he is remembering his mother at her best, being generous with her time, involving herself in loving and fun ways with him when he was young. She was no longer the forever monster mother always criticizing, always aggrieved. She was assuming proportion again in his memories.

His father rearranges himself back on the sofa, placing a large cushion behind him and slowly easing himself against it. He smiles broadly as he notices the familiar etchings. "Your mother's china!" He is quiet for a moment, examining the cups closely. "I'm sorry," he sputters, his voice catching. "It makes me happy to see these again." Confused at himself, he looks up at Jonathan with wondering eyes as if he might know why his emotions are so swift and potent in this moment.

"It's fine, Dad," Jonathan soothes. "I was just thinking myself how much I love having the china set. How much Mom loved it. How she would use it to play with me and Sarah like we were royalty having high tea with the queen."

His father calms himself with sips of hot chocolate. "Mmmm...hits the spot," he remarks, holding his cup up in recognition of Jonathan. He sips again. "You should have seen your mother at her height. Especially when she entertained. Gracious, charming. So damned charming. And yet efficient. Kept things moving. On balance. Just *gliding* around the room taking care of everyone." He takes another sip, gazing far away, gone to some place of his heart where she is still vivacious and alive, not yet disappointed in him, herself, their life. "I loved her," he states simply.

"I know you did," Jonathan sympathetically affirms, looking at his father.

His father is keeping his face down, hidden. But then he meets Jonathan's eyes with a straightforwardness Jonathan has never received. His father is contemplating something. Not speaking but on the verge of it. Jonathan feels a squeeze of dread. He knows the question his father wants to ask. But he's denied the choice to hear or not hear when his father gives shape to it, asking out loud and at last, "Do you think she knew?"

Jonathan is stunned by the convulsing sound escaping his throat.

His father, alarmed, reaches his arm out to him, wanting to pat his hand in comfort. But the violent pain in his lower back as he leans forward defeats him. He shuts his eyes and clenches his teeth.

Now it is Jonathan who is alarmed. He pulls himself back from his outburst. "Are you alright, Dad?"

They look at one another, mirror portraits of torment and grief, silently pondering the other.

"I'm sorry," his father says. "I shouldn't have asked you that. It was unfair."

"No, it wasn't," Jonathan contradicts. "It's just hard thinking about Mom. She suffered a lot in her life, especially in the end. It hurts to know we betrayed her."

"Look at me, Jonny," his father snaps sharply. "I'm the one who betrayed her. Not you. Never you."

Jonathan doesn't want to hear this. Even though he knows it's true, he still feels agitated and uneasy. It has been a long, long time since his father has broached the subject of this period of their lives. But Jonathan remains practiced and calm. He places his fingers tentatively on the side of the pot filled with hot chocolate. "It's still warm." He pours himself a second cup. "You?" he says, pointing the pot at the empty cup in front of his father.

"Yes. Thank you."

Jonathan freshens his father's cocoa. They drink, wary of what to say next. Finally, he asserts, "No. I don't think Mom ever knew what went on between us."

His father sighs heavily. "Even after I got sober, I never considered telling her, to tell you the truth. There were plenty of other things between us to...make right. Then she became so sick. Her cancer saved me from confessing it to her, really. I was a coward, yes, but it did seem unfair, cruel even, to tell her at that point. No matter what she would feel about me, I knew she would be too unforgiving and punishing of herself if she knew what had happened to you."

"Yes. I think you're right about that." Jonathan is resolute. He has often considered the possibility of what his mother may have known about him and his father. She was never at home during their times together, so he doubted she could have had any reason to suspect anything. And she was often blind drunk and oblivious to them all at the time, lost in her own vodka-induced fog. Even in her most brutal and malicious harangues against them both, she never hinted at anything that suggested she knew. She did not know anything of what had happened. He was certain.

She did, however, speak of regrets, her failures and wrongs as a mother, as it became more apparent that she would not get well. Visiting her one day, she requested he guide her to the kitchen table to sit. Once settled, she unequivocally declared, "I'm going to die soon. If there's things you need to say to me, now is the time. I won't stop you or disagree with you. I won't tell you you're wrong. It's OK to let your hate out, Jonathan. I know I earned it. I don't want you living the rest of your life feeling you were never heard by me. I know what bitterness grows when you don't feel heard or seen, especially by your parents. If you never speak up, it stays forever." She spoke plainly and without self-pity.

This was the most prepared for truth she would ever be. And it would be his only chance to tell her how he felt about the many cruel, searingly wounding things she had said and done to him, poisoning his childhood and adolescence. Though he would later wish there had been a better time for him to vomit out all his lacerating remembrances of her humiliating treatment of him, he could not bring himself to say anything to cut her with further regrets or bring her greater suffering. His mother had not taken a drink for nearly two years, and something had purified within her. She was gentler, always expressing gratitude, noting people's kindness in their attention and patience in helping her. She had a softness about her, and he could see glimmers of the shy, innocent, dreaming girl she once was. She was vulnerable. It was many months after her death that he understood she probably always had been.

"There's nothing for me to say. There's nothing for you to say," was his response in that moment. And he meant it at that moment. "You may not have always been a perfect mother, but I was hardly a perfect son," he managed to extract through unwelcomed tears.

"I hope someday you can be honest about how much you hate me. I hope someday your forgiveness of me, and the past, will be genuine. I want to go back to bed now, please." Her abrupt reply was brusque, even irritated—traces of her old unhappy alcoholic self seeping through.

Jonathan was so shocked by her disregard for his tears that he hastily wiped them away and stood up. He placed his mother's rolling walker in front of her and gently elevated her out of the kitchen chair.

They returned to the bedroom. He tenderly aided her back under the blankets. She then asked him to sit beside her. Of course, he did so. They remained there sharing the silence, lost in their own secrets and hells, yet somehow connected. About a half-hour later, she smiled at him and took his hands in hers. This time tears welled up in both their eyes.

"You're a good boy, Jonathan. You'll get there. You will."

And with that, she shut her eyes, tears still streaming, and fell asleep. She died two weeks later, conscious and responsive most of the time, but never again as intimate with him as she was that day.

Jonathan stands holding the silver tray with the china pot and cups. "I better get these cleaned up."

"And I should probably go. It's close to ten," his father says, scooting to the edge of the sofa seat, placing his right arm on its side to leverage himself up. But he doesn't fully make it, the back pain gripping him.

"Don't go yet," Jonathan pleads, startling himself. He's worried about his father, who is in obvious physical pain. But he's also aware that he doesn't want to be abandoned with these memories and the emotions they conjure.

"My goddamned shoulders and back," his father says. "Everything is so tight and knotted. It's awful." His face is contorted in misery, and he seems so pitifully alone.

In a microsecond, a thought leaps into Jonathan's mind, but just as immediately he is able to stop himself from speaking it aloud. Washing the cups, seeming busy and focused, he feels a confused spinning sensation wildly coursing through his body. Jonathan nearly asked his father if he would like for Jonathan to give him a massage.

*What the fuck am I thinking?*

His father once stayed very late on one of their Sunday visits teaching Jonathan various forms of poker for an upcoming Vegas trip with friends. Jonathan had considered asking him to just go ahead and stay overnight instead of making the long drive back to Mountain View, thinking his father could take his bed while he slept on the couch. But on second thought, the idea of giving up his own bed to accommodate the tired man was offensive to Jonathan. Resentment was aroused, even though his father had not alluded to any such adjustment. His father later told him he had not driven far. He had pulled off the highway and checked into a motel in Burlingame as he had almost fallen asleep at the wheel. Jonathan felt waves of self-reproach but knew he had made the right decision then.

He comes around from the kitchen area to the living room and claims the leather chair across from the sofa where his father still sat. Smiling wanly at each other, there was no tension between them. But something was going on, something confusing. Jonathan positively knew it was not sexual, either for his father or himself. But the past had reemerged and pervaded all around them.

More likely, he thought, it never stops pervading all around them. Only tonight, they were at last allowing themselves to notice.

Jonathan recalled how it all had ended—the sex tapered off, was infrequent. The last time they were together, they were clothed, him holding his father. It felt suffocating how pathetic his father was. He doubted if his father's self-loathing even involved him by that point. For all intents and purposes, Jonathan was invisible to him.

There would be a year or two more of onerous drinking before his father decided he wanted—needed—to stop. There was no inpatient rehabilitation treatment for him and no therapist either. Only Alcoholics Anonymous meetings two or three times a day for ten months before they became once or twice a day, continuing even now, except for their Sunday visits. They never attended an AA meeting together.

His father never became a proselytizer for abstention, nor did he make any exertion to convert Jonathan's mother, who kept up her exorbitant alcohol intake without hesitation or apology. She told Jonathan, in one of his last visits with her, that his father had promised he would not interfere with her drinking in any way once he started his recovery. He only asked that she not interfere with his endeavors to stay sober. "It was sort of romantic," she laughed in appreciative irony.

While the initial stages of his father's recovery were taking place, Jonathan was attending college in Boston. This allowed him a valid excuse for staying away. When he returned to the Bay Area nearly a year later, he was unnerved by how much different his father looked and acted after months of not drinking. He seemed older, even worn out, but also clear-eyed and decidedly more present and attentive. He was tentative and timid in his approach to Jonathan. He was legitimately happy to have him home and made strained, sincere efforts to engage in conversations dedicated to Jonathan's academic life and career plans.

But the attendant fallout of the incest was already playing out with Jonathan's own excesses of alcohol and drugs. A messy, chaotic relationship, his first, had ended almost as soon as it started; he now indulged in constant, risky sexual encounters. Wanting to conceal this life, he rebuffed his father with pleasant, manipulative civility.

It was in his penultimate session with the rehab therapist that he finally admitted how it had confused him—*incensed* him, really—that nothing was ever acknowledged when the sex with his father stopped. Just as he had no voice to its beginning, he had no voice to its ending.

"Any explanation I give can only be an excuse," his father's voice intrudes, bolting Jonathan to the present. Just as when he napped and dreamed, it seems his father again has picked up Jonathan's unintended transmission of gnarled memories.

Jonathan practices Dr. Miriam Birnbaum's slow breath exercise as unobtrusively as he can. He needs to steady himself, stay present.

"I was so…impulsive," his father continues. "That's not really the right word. 'Impetuous'? 'Reckless'? I'm sorry, Jonny. There just isn't a word that traps the truth of it. 'Thoughtless' comes closest, I guess. There was no planning or thought. I just did it, and I did it so easily…so…thoughtlessly, that there was no sense of wrong. Afterward, of course, I knew just how wrong, and swore I would never do it again." He strangles back new welling tears. "But once you cross certain lines, you know it can be done." He stops to regain himself. He looks at Jonathan, then around the room, utterly helpless. "I know we've had variations of this conversation before, Jonny, and I know they don't…explain much. Or make much of a difference. But I am sorry, so sorry, for what I did to you."

Jonathan forces himself not to avert his eyes from his father's. He must be unafraid. Unafraid of his once wretched, sometimes still pathetic, always lost father. To be unafraid of the past, and of the future for that matter. Ultimately, for Jonathan to be unafraid of himself.

"You touched yourself," Jonathan says. "That was wrong, yes. But I touched myself too…" His father, upset at what he perceives as Jonathan's self-blame, starts to voice his objection. But Jonathan cuts him off. "I was crossing a line too. A different line, but I did it without thinking also."

"But it was my fault, my doing. I hate what I did to you, Jonny."

"I know you are, Dad. But honestly, at this point, I'm just tired of it all."

His father is weeping faintly. "I wanted to escape my life. I wanted to go back to boyhood. To be a teenage boy again. I was so selfish with you, Jonny. And so weak." His father strikes his clenched fist violently against his own leg.

Jonathan is making himself sit still in the chair, stopping himself from any fidgeting. He maintains control over his breathing. He knows where he wants to go next in this conversation. He is determined to bring himself to that place.

"It's OK, Dad. Really. Stop. No matter what either of us says or does from this point on can change what happened. That's hard to accept. I sometimes still want to get fucked-up drunk about having to accept it. But the longer I go without drinking, the more I get healthy, the more I build my coaching business, the more I…," and here Jonathan hesitated, astonished the words were there for him to speak, "...the more I spend time with you...it just isn't as large as it all once was. It's one of those cliches from my last therapist that makes me want to throw up, but I guess it turns out to be true after all—acceptance of what happened doesn't make what happened acceptable. I've thought about it a lot lately, how people would call me a 'victim' or call me a 'survivor,' and I just don't care anymore. The sex we had, all the stuff around it—the drinking, Mom, dying for affection, maybe even both of us dying for affection—it's a part of my whole life but it's not my whole life itself. I just won't let it be. It can't be. It will be a waste of my life if it's anything more than a part. I'm not going to allow it to be the definition of myself."

"You really are an amazing man, Jonathan," his father whispers, eyes glistening but also brimming with pride.

"Well, there's always a chance tomorrow night I'll be baying at the moon and my skin will be crawling like it's steeped with fire ants, gasping for a drink," Jonathan laughs.

He still has not achieved his destination, but he can wait. He is at peace that he will. They linger in their tranquility a while longer, something feeling settled and clear between them in a way truer than ever before.

At last, his father sighs. "Thank you for all this tonight, Jonathan. Thank you for the entire day, really. It's been...special, very special, to me. A blessing, really."

"Don't go yet, Dad," Jonathan implores. "There's something I need to ask you."

His father returns this statement with a quizzical expression, taken aback that there is something else that needs to be spoken between them. But knowing Jonathan must come first, he encouragingly replies, "Of course. Whatever you need to ask or need to say, I want to listen to."

Jonathan's words come out in a rushing flood. An offer, the thorough details of which he had not even known were there until they are spoken. "Stay and let me give you a massage, Dad. Like I do at the gym. You're hurting so much with your back and shoulders. I'll go slow building up the pressure and depth to dig in and work it out. I'll give you some good long stretches for your legs and lower back to unlock the tension and pain. I'll get you to walking normally again. I can set my table up here in the living room and you can be in your underwear, or I can put a thick blanket over you. I'll be in my t-shirt and long sweatpants I wear at work, so it won't be awkward or weird. I can see how much you need it, Dad, and I'm good at this kind of pain relief massage. Let me help you."

Though he will never be able to accurately, properly describe it to anyone—not even to himself—Jonathan will never forget the innumerable clouds of emotions that shift across his father's face. There is disbelief, almost wonder. Thankfulness, then devastation, bewilderment. And then an ember's flaring of something Jonathan had once seen within his own face when he looked into the mirror at some point during his wrenching journey back to himself. He had stared far into his eyes, as far within himself as he could, refusing to turn away from his reflection until he felt it—a momentary but indisputable defeat of his own unworthiness.

It is at this place his father breaks down, wailing with cries of such woundedness that Jonathan intuitively rushes to him on the sofa and holds him within his arms. Howling in sobs himself, they are bound by something of fathers and sons, parents and children, for which words do not exist and would never be created.

They remained this way a long while. Though exhausted, they pushed themselves to give and receive the massage as Jonathan had outlined. His father discerned it was necessary for him, and even more so for his son, that Jonathan be returned to trust touch between them once again. Fingers, hands, and arms felt, massaged, and kneaded neck and shoulders, back and legs, chest and stomach. No words passed between them. The only sounds were his father's grunts and groans as muscle and sinew were untwisted and released, his body skillfully, methodically, put right.

Bowlfuls of shame had been devoured long enough between them, and the flesh of son upon the flesh of father brought something of healing to both. It mattered little if that healing was of lasting permanence or of mere transience. At least in these hours between them, they had come onto a mystery. One not of Divine, but rather that of human grace.

# Acknowledgments

When compiling this list of Acknowledgements, three people I had not thought of in years resurrected into my consciousness. Or, more accurately, my conscience. The three were long-ago writing teachers. Having made their claim to be recognized for the part they played in my writing life, it is only appropriate to acknowledge them at the beginning.

Sister Robert Clare was the first teacher who recognized my writing and encouraged it, leading me to write a now-lost short story, "He Doesn't Care," which won a little silver medal from a scholastic journal's contest for seventh and eighth graders. The late Dr. Beverly Byers-Pevitts of Kentucky Wesleyan College was impressed enough by a play I wrote to submit it to the editor of *The Best American Short Plays* series. Though it was not accepted, that play made it to a staged reading at an off-off-Broadway theater. The late Dr. Christian Moe at Southern Illinois University of Carbondale gave me the freedom to write about anything I wanted, no matter how explicit or controversial. Some of the plays written under his tutelage went on to be produced or given staged readings in Chicago, Los Angeles, and St. Louis. Our culture still underestimates and undervalues the positive, powerful impact teachers have in changing our lives, and I am grateful to these three for having done so in mine.

The Saints and Sinners Literary Festival in New Orleans deserves recognition for the essential role it has played the past several years—publishing the first short stories I wrote in nearly three decades and providing opportunities to read in front of audiences, pitch book ideas to publishers, and engage in stimulating, purposeful conversations with a number of admired writers I could never imagine myself meeting. Paul J. Willis, the festival's Executive Director, is a classy and kind man who has treated me with the same respect he shows to the major authors in attendance. This simple but meaningful act has made me feel that, yes, I do belong in the world of writers.

Many publishers read the manuscript, offered much praise, and even interest, but always pulled back from taking it on. Ian Henzel and St Sukie de la Croix of Rattling Good Yarns Press, however, did. For that, and so many things, they have my greatest appreciation.

Others who played a part in the book's journey and deserve note are Robert Corrick, who's enthusiasm for "The Last Great Aria of a Magnificent Faggot" assured me I was on the right track; Christopher Hall for his valuable assistance in reading an earlier draft, making suggestions for edits and revisions, and being honest about what he liked and what he did not; and Gordon McClellan, who affirmed I had a book worth publishing. Most importantly, I owe author and friend John Weagly an unpayable debt for his generosity in returning phone calls and emails between years of silence. He would read the stories immediately, volunteer insight and advice, and voice his excitement that I was writing again.

I have been blessed with a deliciously engaging set of friends, many of whom read different versions of the stories over the years and were equally lavish with praise and criticisms that helped me improve them. This group includes David Allison, of the great patience and understanding who also makes me laugh—a lot; Jeffery Byrd, whose constantly expanding creativity and open-hearted sensitivity to the world around him inspires and moves me; Stewart Cunningham, for whom words fail, except to say my life is more fun and far richer because of his presence in it; John Ernst, a bitch, but one of the most thoughtful and charitable bitches I know; Scott Ernst of the good heart; Larry Holben, who bought me shoes; Debi Hopkins, my soul sister since first grade at Immaculate School, and the only person who can draw my attention from across a room and make me laugh out loud with just a look; Trish Glass, the Meryl Streep of Davis community theater who is hilariously, if somewhat scarily, in psychic synch with me about so many things, both of weight and triviality; Nancy and Norbert Greenwell who support me in many ways (and on a couple of occasions, literally!); Jamie Kerrick, my first and best show business-loving gay friend, with whom many dreams were shared and who was unwavering in his faith that someday my stories would find an audience; Bill Kincaid, the director I never had to explain my writing to; Amy Knight, the only work supervisor smarter than me; Phyllis Peters, the best example I know of the committed writer who never gives up; Philip Smith, who reminds me that multiple layers are more important than multiple labels; Cathie Velotta, for special bonds and memories; Jeff Vessels, who shared the risks of being out and gay at a time and place where such risks were rare; and Fred Zapp, who makes me sing.

And to four late friends whose traces on my heart remain—Brother Gabriel Herbig, OSB, Kirk Pamper, Drew Smith, and Patti Terrell—thank you.

It often astonishes me when I consider that I have the privilege to love, and to by loved by, my family. Talented, courageous, delightful, tender-hearted, unstoppable, delicate, compassionate, perceptive, complex, witty, and empathetic are only a starting vocabulary to describe my nephews and nieces,

Nik, Kate, Genny, Amy, and Josh. My life is a happier, fuller one because of them. A special nod to my soon-to-be niece-in-law Christine who gave me the seeds for one of the stories in this collection. And to my sister-in-law Ivy, I shower much praise and affection for how she has made us all a better family. And kept us fed!

As for my sisters Rebecca, Theresa, and Cindi...they are books in and of themselves, and far beyond my talents to ever precisely capture and properly portray. One of their most immeasurable gifts is believing in my writing long after I stopped believing in it myself. *That's* family. I treasure and love them far beyond any vocabulary I possess.

There are too many Westerfields and Hagans now passed to name, but my mother and brother must be honored. My mother, Veronica Genevieve, known best as "Gene," may not have approved of my stories; indeed, they may well have embarrassed and confused her. But I have no doubt she would have been proud and found ways to brag about me having written and published a book. My brother Broni is forever a piece of my soul where joyful, loving, and laughing memories reside with sorrow and grief.

Finally, I thank my late father, Thomas W. ("TW") Westerfield. He was a ten-year Navy veteran, a superb carpenter, a dedicated fireman, and, in 1960, became the first male librarian in the Owensboro-Daviess County, Kentucky public library system. To be honest, I'm not entirely sure if he was *the first*. But it makes for a better story to say he was.

When I was eleven-years old, I showed him a short story I wrote about an evil genius blackmailing the world into behaving better by threatening to blow it up with his own personal atom bomb. After reading it, my father pulled a pen from his shirt pocket. At the top of the page, he wrote out how, if the story was a book, it would be catalogued on a card for the file cabinet where each and every book in the library was listed. For him, it was just a playful, educational moment. But for me, it was a mind-blowing, life-altering one. It was the first time I ever made the connection that something I wrote could be part of that giant, awesome building of endless shelves crammed with books, books, and more books.

More than ever having a book displayed on a bookstore table, I have always dreamed of having a book on a library shelf.

My deepest gratitude to everyone who played a part in making that dream come closer to reality.

# About the Author

Thomas Westerfield's stories have been recognized as a finalist by the Saints and Sinners Festival, the New Millennium Writing Awards for Fiction, and the Dzanc Books Short Story Collection Competition. His plays, *Catharsis* and *Monasteries*, received productions and staged readings in New York City, Los Angeles, Chicago, and San Francisco throughout the 1980s and 1990s. He was recognized as one of the "25 Unsung Heroes of the Gay Community" in 1988 by *The Advocate* magazine for his playwriting and his role in cofounding the Owensboro Gay Alliance in Kentucky.

He currently resides in San Francisco freelancing as a writing consultant while working on his novel *That Goddamned Red Rose*. He is also a certified Laughter Yoga Leader who has conducted sessions for corporate and social service employees, dialysis patients, and seniors living with dementia. His website is thomaswesterfieldwriter.com.